M000201469

HARRY POTTER

AND THE
CURSED CHILD

—◆— PARTS ONE AND TWO —◆—

BASED ON AN ORIGINAL NEW STORY BY

J.K. ROWLING

JOHN TIFFANY & JACK THORNE

A NEW PLAY BY **JACK THORNE**

FIRST PRODUCED BY

SONIA FRIEDMAN PRODUCTIONS, COLIN CALLENDER

& HARRY POTTER THEATRICAL PRODUCTIONS

THE OFFICIAL SCRIPT OF THE

ORIGINAL WEST END PRODUCTION

SPECIAL REHEARSAL EDITION

HARRY POTTER

POTTER

AND THE
CURSED CHILD

—— PARTS ONE AND TWO ——

ARTHUR A. LEVINE BOOKS

AN IMPRINT OF SCHOLASTIC INC.

Text © 2016 by Harry Potter Theatrical Productions Limited
Harry Potter Publishing and Theatrical rights © J.K. Rowling
Artwork and logo are trademarks of and © Harry Potter Theatrical Productions Limited
Harry Potter characters, names, and related indicia are trademarks of and © Warner Bros. Ent.
All rights reserved.
J.K. ROWLING'S WIZARDING WORLD is a trademark of J.K. Rowling and Warner Bros. Entertainment Inc.

All rights reserved. Published by Arthur A. Levine Books, an imprint of Scholastic Inc., *Publishers since 1920.*
SCHOLASTIC and the LANTERN LOGO are trademarks and/or registered trademarks of Scholastic Inc.

The publisher does not have any control over and does not assume any responsibility for author
or third-party websites or their content.

No part of this publication may be reproduced, stored in a retrieval system, or transmitted in any form
or by any means, electronic, mechanical, photocopying, recording, or otherwise, without written
permission of the publisher. For information regarding permission, write to Scholastic Inc.,
Attention: Permissions Department, 557 Broadway, New York, NY 10012.

This book is a work of fiction. Names, characters, places, and incidents are either the product
of the authors' imagination or are used fictitiously, and any resemblance to actual persons, living or dead,
business establishments, events, or locales is entirely coincidental.

**Harry Potter and the Cursed Child Parts One and Two may not be performed in whole or in
part and no use may be made of it whatsoever except under express license from the rights
holders of the work, J.K. Rowling and Harry Potter Theatrical Productions Limited.
Please email inquiries@hptheatricalproductions.com with any inquiries.**

Library of Congress Control Number: 2016944764
ISBN 978-1-338-09913-3
10 9 8 7 6 5 4 3 2 1   16 17 18 19 20
Printed in the U.S.A. at RR Donnelley & Sons, Crawfordsville, Indiana
First edition, July 2016
Book design by Charles Kreloff and David Saylor

MIX
Paper from
responsible sources
FSC® C101537

We try to produce the most beautiful books possible, and we are also extremely concerned
about the impact of our manufacturing process on the forests of the world and the environment as a whole.
Accordingly, we made sure that all of the paper we used contains 30% post-consumer recycled fiber
and has been certified as coming from forests that are managed to insure the protection of the people
and wildlife dependent upon them.

To Jack Thorne
who entered my world
and did beautiful things there.
—J.K. Rowling

For Joe, Louis, Max, Sonny, and Merle . . . wizards all . . .
—John Tiffany

To Elliott Thorne, born April 7, 2016.
As we rehearsed, he gurgled.
—Jack Thorne

CONTENTS

HARRY POTTER

AND THE
CURSED CHILD

— PARTS ONE AND TWO —

HARRY POTTER AND THE CURSED CHILD

PART ONE

ACT ONE

ACT ONE, SCENE ONE

KING'S CROSS

A busy and crowded station. Full of people trying to go somewhere. Amongst the hustle and bustle, two large cages rattle on top of two laden trolleys. They're being pushed by two boys, JAMES POTTER and ALBUS POTTER, their mother, GINNY, follows after. A thirty-seven-year-old man, HARRY, has his daughter, LILY, on his shoulders.

ALBUS: Dad. He keeps saying it.

HARRY: James, give it a rest.

JAMES: I only said he might be in Slytherin. And he might so . . . *(Off his dad's glare.)* Fine.

ALBUS *(looking up at his mum)*: You'll write to me, won't you?

GINNY: Every day if you want us to.

ALBUS: No. Not every day. James says most people only get letters from home about once a month. I don't want to . . .

HARRY: We wrote to your brother three times a week last year.

ALBUS: What? James!

ALBUS looks accusingly at JAMES.

GINNY: Yes. You may not want to believe everything he tells you about Hogwarts. He likes a laugh, your brother.

JAMES *(with a grin)*: Can we go now, please?

ALBUS looks at his dad, and then his mum.

GINNY: All you have to do is walk straight at the wall between platforms nine and ten.

LILY: I'm so excited.

HARRY: Don't stop and don't be scared you'll crash into it, that's very important. Best to do it at a run if you're nervous.

ALBUS: I'm ready.

HARRY and LILY put their hands on ALBUS's trolley — GINNY joins JAMES's trolley — together, the family run hard into the barrier.

ACT ONE, SCENE TWO

PLATFORM NINE AND THREE-QUARTERS

Which is covered in thick white steam pouring from the HOGWARTS EXPRESS.

And which is also busy—but instead of people in sharp suits going about their day—it's now wizards and witches in robes mostly trying to work out how to say good-bye to their beloved progeny.

ALBUS: This is it.

LILY: Wow!

ALBUS: Platform nine and three-quarters.

LILY: Where are they? Are they here? Maybe they didn't come?

> *HARRY points out RON, HERMIONE, and their daughter, ROSE. LILY runs hard up to them.*

> Uncle Ron. Uncle Ron!!!

> *RON turns towards them as LILY goes barreling up to him. He picks her up into his arms.*

RON: If it isn't my favorite Potter.

LILY: Have you got my trick?

RON: Are you aware of the Weasleys' Wizard Wheezes—certified nose-stealing breath?

ROSE: Mum! Dad's doing that lame thing again.

HERMIONE: You say lame, he says glorious, I say—somewhere in between.

RON: Hang on. Let me just munch this . . . air. And now it's just a simple matter of . . . Excuse me if I smell slightly of garlic . . .

He breathes on her face. LILY giggles.

LILY: You smell of porridge.

RON: Bing. Bang. Boing. Young lady, get ready to not being able to smell at all . . .

He lifts her nose off.

LILY: Where's my nose?

RON: Ta-da!

His hand is empty. It's a lame trick. Everyone enjoys its lameness.

LILY: You are silly.

ALBUS: Everyone's staring at us again.

RON: Because of me! I'm extremely famous. My nose experiments are legendary!

HERMIONE: They're certainly something.

HARRY: Parked all right, then?

PART ONE

RON: I did. Hermione didn't believe I could pass a Muggle driving test, did you? She thought I'd have to Confund the examiner.

HERMIONE: I thought nothing of the kind, I have complete faith in you.

ROSE: And I have complete faith he did Confund the examiner.

RON: Oi!

ALBUS: Dad . . .

ALBUS pulls on HARRY's robes. HARRY looks down.

Do you think — what if I am — what if I'm put in Slytherin . . .

HARRY: And what would be wrong with that?

ALBUS: Slytherin is the House of the snake, of Dark Magic . . . It's not a House of brave wizards.

HARRY: Albus Severus, you were named after two headmasters of Hogwarts. One of them was a Slytherin and he was probably the bravest man I ever knew.

ALBUS: But just say . . .

HARRY: If it matters to you, *you*, the Sorting Hat will take your feelings into account.

ALBUS: Really?

HARRY: It did for me.

This is something he's never said before, it resonates around his head a moment.

Hogwarts will be the making of you, Albus. I promise you, there is nothing to be frightened of there.

JAMES: Apart from the Thestrals. Watch out for the Thestrals.

ALBUS: I thought they were invisible!

HARRY: Listen to your professors, *don't* listen to James, and remember to enjoy yourself. Now, if you don't want this train to leave without you, you should leap on . . .

LILY: I'm going to chase the train out.

GINNY: Lily, come straight back.

HERMIONE: Rose. Remember to send Neville our love.

ROSE: Mum, I can't give a professor love!

ROSE exits for the train. And then ALBUS turns and hugs GINNY and HARRY one last time before following after her.

ALBUS: Okay, then. Bye.

He climbs on board. HERMIONE, GINNY, RON, and HARRY stand watching the train — as whistles blow up and down the platform.

GINNY: They're going to be okay, right?

HERMIONE: Hogwarts is a big place.

RON: Big. Wonderful. Full of food. I'd give anything to be going back.

HARRY: Strange, Al being worried he'll be sorted into Slytherin.

HERMIONE: That's nothing, Rose is worried whether she'll break the Quidditch scoring record in her first or second year. And how early she can take her O.W.L.s.

RON: I have no idea where she gets her ambition from.

GINNY: And how would you feel, Harry, if Al—if he is?

RON: You know, Gin, we always thought there was a chance you could be sorted into Slytherin.

GINNY: What?

RON: Honestly, Fred and George ran a book.

HERMIONE: Can we go? People are looking, you know.

GINNY: People always look when you three are together. And apart. People always look at you.

The four exit. GINNY stops HARRY.

Harry . . . He'll be all right, won't he?

HARRY: Of course he will.

ACT ONE, SCENE THREE

THE HOGWARTS EXPRESS

ALBUS and ROSE walk along the carriage of the train.

The TROLLEY WITCH approaches, pushing her trolley.

TROLLEY WITCH: Anything from the trolley, dears? Pumpkin Pasty? Chocolate Frog? Cauldron Cake?

ROSE *(spotting ALBUS's loving look at the Chocolate Frogs)*: Al. We need to concentrate.

ALBUS: Concentrate on what?

ROSE: On who we choose to be friends with. My mum and dad met your dad on their first Hogwarts Express, you know . . .

ALBUS: So we need to choose now who to be friends with for life? That's quite scary.

ROSE: On the contrary, it's exciting. I'm a Granger-Weasley, you're a Potter — everyone will want to be friends with us, we've got the pick of anyone we want.

ALBUS: So how do we decide — which compartment to go in . . .

ROSE: We rate them all and then we make a decision.

ALBUS opens a door—to look in on a lonely blond kid—SCORPIUS—in an otherwise empty compartment. ALBUS smiles. SCORPIUS smiles back.

ALBUS: Hi. Is this compartment . . .

SCORPIUS: It's free. It's just me.

ALBUS: Great. So we might just—come in—for a bit—if that's okay?

SCORPIUS: That's okay. Hi.

ALBUS: Albus. Al. I'm—my name is Albus . . .

SCORPIUS: Hi Scorpius. I mean, I'm Scorpius. You're Albus. I'm Scorpius. And you must be . . .

ROSE's face is growing colder by the minute.

ROSE: Rose.

SCORPIUS: Hi, Rose. Would you like some of my Fizzing Whizbees?

ROSE: I've just had breakfast, thanks.

SCORPIUS: I've also got some Shock-o-Choc, Pepper Imps, and some Jelly Slugs. Mum's idea—she says *(sings)*, "Sweets, they always help you make friends." *(He realizes that singing was a mistake.)* Stupid idea, probably.

ALBUS: I'll have some . . . Mum doesn't let me have sweets. Which one would you start with?

ROSE hits ALBUS out of sight of SCORPIUS.

SCORPIUS: Easy. I've always regarded the Pepper Imp as the king of the confectionery bag. They're peppermint sweets that make you smoke at the ears.

ALBUS: Brilliant, then that's what I'll— *(ROSE hits him again.)* Rose, will you please stop hitting me?

ROSE: I'm not hitting you.

ALBUS: You *are* hitting me, and it hurts.

SCORPIUS's face falls.

SCORPIUS: She's hitting you because of me.

ALBUS: What?

SCORPIUS: Listen, I know who you are, so it's probably only fair you know who I am.

ALBUS: What do you mean you know who I am?

SCORPIUS: You're Albus Potter. She's Rose Granger-Weasley. And I am Scorpius Malfoy. My parents are Astoria and Draco Malfoy. Our parents—they didn't get on.

ROSE: That's putting it mildly. Your mum and dad are Death Eaters!

SCORPIUS *(affronted)*: Dad was—but Mum wasn't.

ROSE looks away, and SCORPIUS knows why she does.

I know what the rumor is, and it's a lie.

ALBUS looks from an uncomfortable ROSE to a desperate SCORPIUS.

ALBUS: What—is the rumor?

SCORPIUS: The *rumor* is that my parents couldn't have children. That my father and my grandfather were so desperate for a powerful heir, to prevent the end of the Malfoy line, that they . . . that they used a Time-Turner to send my mother back . . .

ALBUS: To send her back where?

ROSE: The rumor is that he's Voldemort's son, Albus.

A horrible, uncomfortable silence.

It's probably rubbish. I mean . . . look, you've got a nose.

The tension is slightly broken. SCORPIUS laughs, pathetically grateful.

SCORPIUS: And it's just like my father's! I got his nose, his hair, and his name. Not that that's a great thing either. I mean—father-son issues, I have them. But, on the whole, I'd rather be a Malfoy than, you know, the son of the Dark Lord.

SCORPIUS and ALBUS look at each other and something passes between them.

ROSE: Yes, well, we probably should sit somewhere else. Come on, Albus.

ALBUS is thinking deeply.

ALBUS: No. *(Off ROSE's look.)* I'm okay. You go on . . .

ROSE: Albus. I won't wait.

ALBUS: And I wouldn't expect you to. But I'm staying here.

ROSE looks at him a second and then leaves the compartment.

ROSE: Fine!

SCORPIUS and ALBUS are left—looking at each other—unsure.

SCORPIUS: Thank you.

ALBUS: No. No. I didn't stay — for you — I stayed for your sweets.

SCORPIUS: She's quite fierce.

ALBUS: Yes. Sorry.

SCORPIUS: No. I like it. Do you prefer Albus or Al?

SCORPIUS grins and pops two sweets into his mouth.

ALBUS *(thinks)*: Albus.

SCORPIUS *(as smoke comes out of his ears)*: THANK YOU FOR STAYING FOR MY SWEETS, ALBUS!

ALBUS *(laughing)*: Wow.

ACT ONE, SCENE FOUR

TRANSITION SCENE

And now we enter a never-world of time change. And this scene is all *about magic. The changes are rapid as we leap between worlds. There are no individual scenes, but fragments, shards that show the constant progression of time.*

Initially we're inside Hogwarts, in the Great Hall, and everyone is dancing around ALBUS.

POLLY CHAPMAN: Albus Potter.

KARL JENKINS: A Potter. In our year.

YANN FREDERICKS: He's got his hair. He's got hair just like him.

ROSE: And he's my cousin. *(As they turn.)* Rose Granger-Weasley. Nice to meet you.

> *The SORTING HAT walks through the students, who spring into their Houses.*
>
> *It becomes quickly apparent he's approaching ROSE, who is tense as she awaits her fate.*

SORTING HAT: I've done this job for centuries
On every student's head I've sat

Of thoughts I take inventories
For I'm the famous Sorting Hat

I've sorted high, I've sorted low,
I've done the job through thick and thin
So put me on and you will know
Which House you should be in . . .
Rose Granger-Weasley.

He puts his hat on ROSE's head.

GRYFFINDOR!

There's cheering from the Gryffindors as ROSE joins them.

ROSE: Thank Dumbledore.

SCORPIUS runs to take ROSE's place under the SORTING HAT's glare.

SORTING HAT: Scorpius Malfoy.

He puts his hat on SCORPIUS's head.

SLYTHERIN!

SCORPIUS was expecting this, he nods and half smiles. There's cheering from the Slytherins as he joins them.

POLLY CHAPMAN: Well, that makes sense.

ALBUS walks swiftly to the front of the stage.

SORTING HAT: Albus Potter.

He puts his hat on ALBUS's head — and this time he seems to take longer — almost as if he too is confused.

SLYTHERIN!

There's a silence.

A perfect, profound silence.

One that sits low, twists a bit, and has damage within it.

POLLY CHAPMAN: Slytherin?

CRAIG BOWKER JR.: Whoa! A Potter? In Slytherin.

ALBUS looks out, unsure. SCORPIUS smiles, delighted, as he shouts across to him.

SCORPIUS: You can stand next to me!

ALBUS *(thoroughly discombobulated)*: Right. Yes.

YANN FREDERICKS: I suppose his hair isn't that similar.

ROSE: Albus? But this is wrong, Albus. This is not how it's supposed to be.

And suddenly a flying lesson is happening with MADAM HOOCH.

MADAM HOOCH: Well, what are you all waiting for? Everyone stand by a broomstick. Come on, hurry up.

The kids all hurry into position beside their brooms.

Stick out your hands out over your broom, and say, "Up!"

EVERYONE: UP!

ROSE's and YANN's brooms sail into their hands.

ROSE and YANN: Yes!

MADAM HOOCH: Come on, now, I've no time for shirkers. Say "UP." "UP" like you mean it.

EVERYONE *(bar ROSE and YANN)*: UP!

Brooms sail up, including SCORPIUS's. Only ALBUS is left with his broom on the floor.

EVERYONE *(bar ROSE, YANN, and ALBUS)*: YES!

ALBUS: Up. UP. UP.

His broom doesn't move. Not even a millimeter. He stares at it with disbelieving desperation. There's giggling from the rest of the class.

POLLY CHAPMAN: Oh Merlin's beard, how humiliating! He really isn't like his father at all, is he?

KARL JENKINS: Albus Potter, the Slytherin Squib.

MADAM HOOCH: Okay. Children. Time to fly.

And suddenly HARRY appears from nowhere beside ALBUS as steam expands all over the stage.

We're back on platform nine and three-quarters and time has ticked on mercilessly. ALBUS is now a year older (as is HARRY, but less noticeably).

ALBUS: I'm just asking you, Dad, if you'll—if you'll just stand a little away from me.

HARRY *(amused)*: Second-years don't like to be seen with their dads, is that it?

An OVER-ATTENTIVE WIZARD begins to circle them.

ALBUS: No. It's just—you're *you* and—and I'm me and—

HARRY: It's just people looking, okay? People look. And they're looking at me, not you.

><+❖>+<

The OVER-ATTENTIVE WIZARD proffers something for HARRY to sign — he signs it.

ALBUS: At Harry Potter and his disappointing son.

HARRY: What does that mean?

ALBUS: At Harry Potter and his Slytherin son.

JAMES rushes past them, carrying his bag.

JAMES: Slythering Slytherin, stop with your dithering, time to get onto the train.

HARRY: Unnecessary, James.

JAMES *(long gone)*: See you at Christmas, Dad.

HARRY looks at ALBUS, concerned.

HARRY: Al—

ALBUS: My name is Albus, not Al.

HARRY: Are the other kids being unkind? Is that it? Maybe if you tried making a few more friends . . . without Hermione and Ron I wouldn't have survived Hogwarts, I wouldn't have survived at all.

ALBUS: But I don't need a Ron and Hermione. I've — I've got a friend, Scorpius, and I know you don't like him but he's all I need.

HARRY: Look, as long as you're happy, that's all that matters to me.

ALBUS: You didn't need to bring me to the station, Dad.

ALBUS picks up his case and makes hard away.

HARRY: But I *wanted* to be here . . .

But ALBUS is gone. DRACO MALFOY, his robes perfect, his blond ponytail precisely placed, emerges from within the crowds to be beside HARRY.

DRACO: I need a favor.

HARRY: Draco.

DRACO: These rumors—about my son's parentage—they don't seem to be going away. The other Hogwarts students tease Scorpius about it relentlessly—if the Ministry could release a statement reaffirming that all Time-Turners were destroyed in the Battle of the Department of Mysteries . . .

HARRY: Draco, just let it blow over—they'll soon move on.

DRACO: My son is suffering and—Astoria hasn't been well recently—so he needs all the support he can get.

HARRY: If you answer the gossip, you feed the gossip. There've been rumors Voldemort had a child for years, Scorpius is not the first to be accused. The Ministry, for your sake as well as ours, needs to steer well clear.

DRACO frowns, annoyed, as the stage clears and ROSE and ALBUS stand ready with their cases.

ALBUS: As soon as the train leaves you don't have to talk to me.

ROSE: I know. We just need to keep the pretense up in front of the grown-ups.

SCORPIUS runs on—with big hopes and an even bigger case.

SCORPIUS *(hopeful)*: Hi, Rose.

ROSE *(definitive)*: Bye, Albus.

SCORPIUS *(still hopeful)*: She's melting.

And suddenly we're in the Great Hall and PROFESSOR McGONAGALL is standing at the front with a big smile on her face.

PROFESSOR McGONAGALL: And I'm pleased to announce Gryffindor's newest member of the Quidditch team—our—*(she realizes she can't be partial)* your superb new Chaser—Rose Granger-Weasley.

The hall erupts into cheers. SCORPIUS claps alongside them all.

ALBUS: Are you clapping her too? We hate Quidditch and she's playing for another House.

SCORPIUS: She's your cousin, Albus.

ALBUS: Do you think she'd clap for me?

SCORPIUS: I think she's brilliant.

The students circle ALBUS again as suddenly a Potions class begins.

POLLY CHAPMAN: Albus Potter. An irrelevance. Even portraits turn the other way when he comes up the stairs.

ALBUS hunches over a potion.

ALBUS: And now we add—is it horn of bicorn?

KARL JENKINS: Leave him and Voldemort's child to it, I say.

ALBUS: With just a little salamander blood . . .

The potion explodes loudly.

SCORPIUS: Okay. What's the counter-ingredient? What do we need to change?

ALBUS: Everything.

And with that, time moves ever onwards—ALBUS's eyes become darker, his face grows more sallow. He's still an attractive boy, but he's trying not to admit it.

And suddenly he's back on platform nine and three-quarters with his dad—who is still trying to persuade his son (and himself) that everything is okay. Both have aged another year.

HARRY: Third year. Big year. Here is your permission form for Hogsmeade.

ALBUS: I hate Hogsmeade.

HARRY: How can you hate a place you haven't actually visited yet?

ALBUS: Because I know it'll be full of Hogwarts students.

ALBUS screws up the paper.

HARRY: Just give it a go—come on—this is your chance to go nuts in Honeydukes without your mum knowing—no, Albus, don't you dare.

ALBUS *(pointing his wand)*: Incendio!

The ball of paper bursts into flame and ascends across the stage.

HARRY: Of all the stupid things!

ALBUS: The ironic thing is I didn't expect it to work. I'm terrible at that spell.

HARRY: Al—Albus, I've been exchanging owls with Professor McGonagall—she says you're isolating yourself—you're uncooperative in lessons—you're surly—you're—

ALBUS: So what would you like me to do? Magic myself popular? Conjure myself into a new House? Transfigure myself into a better student? Just cast a spell, Dad, and change me into what you want me to be, okay? It'll work better for both of us. Got to go. Train to catch. Friend to find.

ALBUS runs to SCORPIUS, who is sitting on his case—numb to the world.

(*Delighted.*) Scorpius . . . (*Concerned.*) Scorpius . . . Are you okay?

SCORPIUS says nothing. ALBUS tries to read his friend's eyes.

Your mum? It's got worse?

SCORPIUS: It's got the worst it can possibly get.

ALBUS sits down beside SCORPIUS.

ALBUS: I thought you'd send an owl . . .

SCORPIUS: I couldn't work out what to say.

ALBUS: And now I don't know what to say . . .

SCORPIUS: Say nothing.

ALBUS: Is there anything . . . ?

SCORPIUS: Come to the funeral.

ALBUS: Of course.

SCORPIUS: And be my good friend.

And suddenly the SORTING HAT is center stage and we're back in the Great Hall.

SORTING HAT: Are you afraid of what you'll hear?
　　　　　　Afraid I'll speak the name you fear?
　　　　　　Not Slytherin! Not Gryffindor!
　　　　　　Not Hufflepuff! Not Ravenclaw!
　　　　　　Don't worry, child, I know my job,
　　　　　　You'll learn to laugh, if first you sob.
　　　　　　Lily Potter. GRYFFINDOR.

LILY: Yes!

ALBUS: Great.

SCORPIUS: Did you really think she'd come to us? Potters don't belong in Slytherin.

ALBUS: This one does.

As he tries to melt into the background, the other students laugh. He looks up at them all.

I didn't choose, you know that? I didn't choose to be his son.

ACT ONE, SCENE FIVE

MINISTRY OF MAGIC, HARRY'S OFFICE

HERMIONE sits with piles of paper in front of her in HARRY's messy office. She is slowly sorting through it all. HARRY enters in a rush. He is bleeding from a graze on his cheek.

HERMIONE: How did it go?

HARRY: It was true.

HERMIONE: Theodore Nott?

HARRY: In custody.

HERMIONE: And the Time-Turner itself?

> *HARRY reveals the Time-Turner. It shines out alluringly.*

> Is it genuine? Does it work? It's not just an hour-reversal turner — it goes back further?

HARRY: We don't know anything yet. I wanted to try it out there and then but wiser heads prevailed.

HERMIONE: Well, now we have it.

HARRY: And you're sure you want to keep it?

HERMIONE: I don't think we've a choice. Look at it. It's entirely different to the Time-Turner I had.

HARRY *(dry)*: Apparently wizardry has moved on since we were kids.

HERMIONE: You're bleeding.

> *HARRY checks his face in the mirror. He dabs at the wound with his robes.*

Don't worry, it'll go with the scar.

HARRY *(with a grin)*: What you doing in my office, Hermione?

HERMIONE: I was anxious to hear about Theodore Nott and — thought I'd check whether you'd kept your promise and were on top of your paperwork.

HARRY: Ah. Turns out I'm not.

HERMIONE: No. You're not. Harry, how can you get any work done in this chaos?

> *HARRY waves his wand and the papers and books transform into neat piles. HARRY smiles.*

HARRY: No longer chaotic.

HERMIONE: But still ignored. You know, there's some interesting stuff in here . . . There are mountain trolls riding Graphorns through Hungary, there are giants with winged tattoos on their backs walking through the Greek Seas, and the werewolves have gone entirely underground —

HARRY: Great, let's get out there. I'll get the team together.

HERMIONE: Harry, I get it. Paperwork's boring . . .

HARRY: Not for you.

HERMIONE: I'm busy enough with my own. These are people and beasts that fought alongside Voldemort in the great wizarding wars. These are allies of darkness. This—combined with what we have just unearthed at Theodore Nott's—could mean something. But if the Head of Magical Law Enforcement isn't reading his files—

HARRY: But I don't need to read it—I'm out there, hearing about it. Theodore Nott—it was me who heard the rumors about the Time-Turner and me who acted upon it. You really don't need to tell me off.

HERMIONE looks at HARRY—this is tricky.

HERMIONE: Do you fancy a toffee? Don't tell Ron.

HARRY: You're changing the subject.

HERMIONE: I truly am. Toffee?

HARRY: Can't. We're off sugar at the moment. *(Beat.)* You know, you can get addicted to that stuff?

HERMIONE: What can I say? My parents were dentists, I was bound to rebel at some point. Forty is leaving it a little late, but . . . You've just done a brilliant thing. You're certainly not being told off— I just need you to look at your paperwork every now and again, that's all. Consider this a gentle—nudge—from *the Minister for Magic.*

HARRY hears the implication in her emphasis, he nods.

How's Ginny? How's Albus?

HARRY: It seems I'm as good at fatherhood as I am at paperwork. How's Rose? How's Hugo?

HERMIONE *(with a grin)*: You know, Ron says he thinks I see more of my secretary, Ethel, *(she indicates off)* than him. Do you think there's a point where we made a choice—parent of the year or Ministry official of the year? Go on. Go home to your family, Harry, the Hogwarts Express is about to depart for another year—enjoy the time you've got left—and then come back here with a fresh head and get these files read.

HARRY: You really think this could all mean something?

HERMIONE *(with a smile)*: It could do. But if it does, we'll find a way to fight it, Harry. We always have.

She smiles once more, pops a toffee in her mouth, and leaves the office. HARRY is left alone. He packs his bag. He walks out of the office and down a corridor. The weight of the world upon his shoulders.

He walks, tired, into a telephone box. He dials 62442.

TELEPHONE BOX: Farewell, Harry Potter.

He ascends away from the Ministry of Magic.

PART ONE

ACT ONE, SCENE SIX

HARRY AND GINNY POTTER'S HOUSE

ALBUS can't sleep. He is sitting at the top of the stairs. He hears voices below him. We hear HARRY's voice before he's revealed. An elderly man in a wheelchair is with him, AMOS DIGGORY.

HARRY: Amos, I understand, I really do—but I'm only just home and—

AMOS: I've tried to make appointments at the Ministry. They say, "Ah, Mr. Diggory, we have an appointment for you, let's see, in two months." I wait. Very patiently.

HARRY: —and coming to my house in the middle of the night—when my kids are just getting ready for their new year at school—it's not right.

AMOS: Two months pass, I receive an owl, "Mr. Diggory, I'm awfully sorry, but Mr. Potter has been called away on urgent business, we're going to have to shift things around a little, are you available for an appointment in, let's see, in two months' time." And then it repeats again, and again . . . You're shutting me out.

HARRY: Of course I'm not. It's just, I'm afraid, as Head of the Department of Magical Law Enforcement I'm afraid I'm responsible —

AMOS: There's plenty you're responsible for.

HARRY: Sorry?

AMOS: My son, Cedric, you do remember Cedric, don't you?

HARRY *(remembering Cedric hurts him)*: Yes, I remember your son. His loss —

AMOS: Voldemort wanted you! Not my son! You told me yourself, the words he said were, "Kill the spare." The spare. My son, my beautiful son, was a spare.

HARRY: Mr. Diggory, as you know, I sympathize with your efforts to memorialize Cedric, but —

AMOS: A memorial? I am not interested in a memorial — not anymore. I am an old man — an old dying man — and I am here to ask you — beg you — to help me get him back.

HARRY looks up, astonished.

HARRY: Get him back? Amos, that's not possible.

AMOS: The Ministry has a Time-Turner, does it not?

HARRY: The Time-Turners were all destroyed.

AMOS: The reason I'm here with such urgency is I've just heard rumor — strong rumor — that the Ministry seized an illegal Time-Turner from Theodore Nott and has kept it. For investigation. Let me use that Time-Turner. Let me have my son back.

~❖~

There's a long, deadly pause. HARRY is finding this extremely difficult. We watch as ALBUS moves closer, listening.

HARRY: Amos, playing with Time? You know we can't do that.

AMOS: How many people have died for the Boy Who Lived? I'm asking you to save one of them.

This hurts HARRY. He thinks, his face hardens.

HARRY: Whatever you've heard, the Theodore Nott story is a fiction, Amos, I'm sorry.

DELPHI: Hello.

ALBUS jumps a mile as DELPHI — a twenty-something, determined-looking woman — is revealed, looking through the stairs at him.

Oh. Sorry. Didn't mean to startle. I used to be a big stair-listener myself. Sitting there. Waiting for someone to say something the tiniest bit interesting.

ALBUS: Who are you? Because this is sort of my house and . . .

DELPHI: I'm a thief, of course. I'm about to steal everything you own. Give me your gold, your wand, and your Chocolate Frogs! *(She looks fierce and then smiles.)* Either that or I'm Delphini Diggory. *(She ascends the stairs and sticks out a hand.)* Delphi. I look after him — Amos — well, I try. *(She indicates AMOS.)* And you are?

ALBUS *(rueful grin)*: Albus.

DELPHI: Of course! Albus Potter! So Harry is your dad? That's a bit wow, isn't it?

ALBUS: Not really.

DELPHI: Ah. Have I just put my foot in it? It's what they used to say about me at school. Delphini Diggory—there isn't a hole she couldn't dig herself into.

ALBUS: They do all sorts with my name too.

Pause. She looks at him carefully.

AMOS: Delphi.

She makes to depart and then hesitates. She smiles at ALBUS.

DELPHI: We don't choose who we're related to. Amos . . . isn't just my patient, he's my uncle, it's part of the reason I took the job at Upper Flagley. But that's made it difficult. It's tough to live with people stuck in the past, isn't it?

AMOS: Delphi!

ALBUS: Upper Flagley?

DELPHI: St. Oswald's Home for Old Witches and Wizards. Come see us sometime. If you like.

AMOS: DELPHI!

She smiles and then trips as she travels down the stairs. She enters the room with AMOS and HARRY in it. ALBUS watches her.

DELPHI: Yes, Uncle?

AMOS: Meet the once-great Harry Potter, now a stone-cold Ministry man. I will leave you in peace, sir. If peace is the right word for it. Delphi, my chair . . .

DELPHI: Yes, Uncle.

AMOS is pushed out of the room. HARRY is left, looking forlorn. ALBUS watches on, thinking carefully.

ACT ONE, SCENE SEVEN

HARRY AND GINNY POTTER'S HOUSE,
ALBUS'S ROOM

ALBUS is sitting on the bed as the world goes on outside his door. Still against the constant motion outside. We hear a roar from JAMES (off).

GINNY: James, please, ignore your hair, and tidy that damn room . . .

JAMES: How can I ignore it? It's pink! I'm going to have to use my Invisibility Cloak!

JAMES appears at the door, he has pink hair.

GINNY: That's *not* why your dad gave you that Cloak!

LILY: Who's seen my Potions book?

GINNY: Lily Potter, don't think you're wearing those to school tomorrow . . .

LILY appears at ALBUS's door. She's wearing fairy wings that flutter.

LILY: I love them. They're fluttery.

She exits as HARRY appears in ALBUS's doorway. He looks through.

✦

HARRY: Hi.

There's an awkward pause between them. GINNY appears in the doorway. She sees what's happening, she stays a moment.

Just delivering a pre-Hogwarts gift — gifts — Ron's sent this . . .

ALBUS: Okay. A love potion. Okay.

HARRY: I think it's a joke about — I don't know what. Lily got farting gnomes, James got a comb that's made his hair turn a shade of pink. Ron — well, Ron's Ron, you know?

HARRY puts down ALBUS's love potion on his bed.

I also — this is from me . . .

He reveals a small blanket. GINNY looks at it, she sees HARRY is trying, and then she softly walks away.

ALBUS: An old blanket?

HARRY: I thought a lot about what to give you this year. James — well, James has been going on about the Invisibility Cloak since time itself, and Lily — I knew she'd love wings — but you. You're fourteen years old now, Albus, and I wanted to give you something which — meant something. This . . . is the last thing I had from my mum. The only thing. I was given to the Dursleys wrapped in it. I thought it had gone forever and then, when your great-aunt Petunia died, hidden amongst her possessions, surprisingly, Dudley found this and he kindly sent it on to me, and ever since then — well, anytime I've wanted luck I've found it and just tried to hold it and I wondered if you . . .

ALBUS: Wanted to hold it too? Okay. Done. Let's hope it brings me luck. I certainly need some.

He touches the blanket.

But you should keep it.

HARRY: I think—believe—Petunia wanted me to have it, that's why she kept it, and now I want you to have it from me. I didn't really know my mother—but I think she'd have wanted you to have it too. And maybe—I could come find you—and it—on Hallows' Eve. I'd like to be with it on the night they died—and that could be good for the two of us . . .

ALBUS: Listen, I've got quite a lot of packing to do, and you undoubtedly have Ministry work coming out of your ears, so . . .

HARRY: Albus, I want you to have the blanket.

ALBUS: And do what with it? Fairy wings make sense, Dad, invisibility cloaks, they also make sense—but this—really?

HARRY is slightly heartbroken. He looks at his son, desperate to reach out.

HARRY: Do you want a hand? Packing. I always loved packing. It meant I was leaving Privet Drive and going back to Hogwarts. Which was . . . well, I know you don't love it but . . .

ALBUS: For you, it's the greatest place on earth. I know. The poor orphan, bullied by his uncle and aunt Dursley . . .

HARRY: Albus, please—can we just—

ALBUS: . . . traumatized by his cousin, Dudley, saved by Hogwarts. I know it all, Dad. Blah, blah, blah.

HARRY: I'm not going to rise to your bait, Albus Potter.

ALBUS: The poor orphan who went on to save us all. So may I say — on behalf of wizarding kind — how grateful we are for your heroism. Should we bow now or will a curtsy do?

HARRY: Albus, please — you know, I've never wanted gratitude.

ALBUS: But right now I'm overflowing with it — it must be the kind gift of this moldy blanket that did it . . .

HARRY: Moldy blanket?

ALBUS: What did you think would happen? We'd hug. I'd tell you I always loved you. What? What?

HARRY (*finally losing his temper*): You know what? I'm done with being made responsible for your unhappiness. At least you've got a dad. Because I didn't, okay?

ALBUS: And you think that was unlucky? I don't.

HARRY: You wish me dead?

ALBUS: No! I just wish you weren't my dad.

HARRY (*seeing red*): Well, there are times I wish you weren't my son.

There's a silence. ALBUS nods. Pause. HARRY realizes what he's said.

No, I didn't mean that . . .

ALBUS: Yes. You did.

HARRY: Albus, you just know how to get under my skin . . .

ALBUS: You meant it, Dad. And, honestly, I don't blame you.

There's a horrible pause.

You should probably leave me alone now.

HARRY: Albus, please . . .

ALBUS picks up the blanket and throws it. It collides with RON's love potion, which spills all over the blanket and the bed, producing a small puff of smoke.

ALBUS: No luck or love for me, then.

ALBUS runs out of the room. HARRY goes after him.

HARRY: Albus. Albus . . . Please . . .

ACT ONE, SCENE EIGHT

DREAM, HUT-ON-THE-ROCK

There's a LARGE BOOM. Then there's a LARGE CRASH. DUDLEY DURSLEY, AUNT PETUNIA, and UNCLE VERNON are cowering behind a bed.

DUDLEY DURSLEY: Mum, I don't like this.

AUNT PETUNIA: I knew we made a mistake coming here. Vernon. Vernon. There's nowhere we can hide. Not even a lighthouse is far enough away!

There's another LARGE BOOM.

UNCLE VERNON: Hold on. Hold on. Whatever it is, it's not coming in here.

AUNT PETUNIA: We're cursed! He's cursed us! The boy has cursed us! *(Seeing YOUNG HARRY.)* This is all your fault. Get back in your hole.

YOUNG HARRY flinches away as UNCLE VERNON holds out his rifle.

UNCLE VERNON: Whoever's there, I should warn you — I'm armed.

There's a MASSIVE SMASH. And the door falls off its hinges. HAGRID stands in the middle of the doorway. He looks at them all.

HAGRID: Couldn't make us a cup o' tea, could yeh? It's not been an easy journey.

DUDLEY DURSLEY: Look. At. Him.

UNCLE VERNON: Stand back. Stand back. Behind me, Petunia. Behind me, Dudley. I'll soon see this scarramanger off.

HAGRID: Scarrawhat?

He picks up UNCLE VERNON's gun.

Haven't seen one of these for a while.

He twists the end of the gun and ties it in a knot.

Oops-a-daisy.

And then he gets distracted. He's seen YOUNG HARRY.

Harry Potter.

YOUNG HARRY: Hello.

HAGRID: Las' time I saw yeh, yeh was only a baby. Yeh look a lot like yer dad, but yeh've got yer mum's eyes.

YOUNG HARRY: You knew my parents?

HAGRID: Where's me manners? A very happy birthday to yeh. Got summat fer yeh here—I mighta sat on it at some point, but it'll taste all right.

From inside his coat he pulls a slightly squashed chocolate cake with "Happy Birthday Harry" written on it in green icing.

YOUNG HARRY: Who are you?

꾸❖꾸

HAGRID *(laughing)*: True, I haven't introduced meself. Rubeus Hagrid, Keeper of Keys and Grounds at Hogwarts. *(He looks around himself.)* What about that tea, then, eh? I'd not say no ter summat stronger if yeh've got it, mind.

YOUNG HARRY: Hogwhere?

HAGRID: Hogwarts. Yeh'll know all about Hogwarts, o' course.

YOUNG HARRY: Er—no. Sorry.

HAGRID: Sorry? It's them as should be sorry! I knew yeh weren't gettin' yer letters but I never thought yeh wouldn't even know abou' Hogwarts, fer cryin' out loud! Did yeh never wonder where yer parents learnt it all?

YOUNG HARRY: Learnt what?

HAGRID turns menacingly towards UNCLE VERNON.

HAGRID: Do you mean ter tell me, that this boy—this boy!—knows nothin' abou'—about ANYTHING?

UNCLE VERNON: I forbid you to tell the boy anything more!

YOUNG HARRY: Tell me what?

HAGRID looks at UNCLE VERNON and then at YOUNG HARRY.

HAGRID: Harry—yer a wizard—yeh changed everything. Yer the most famous wizard in the whole world.

And then, right from the back of the room, whispering around everyone.

Words said with an unmistakable voice. The voice of VOLDEMORT . . .

Haaarry Pottttter.

ACT ONE, SCENE NINE

HARRY AND GINNY POTTER'S HOUSE, BEDROOM

HARRY wakes suddenly. Breathing deeply in the night.

He waits a moment. Calming himself. And then he feels intense pain in his forehead. In his scar. Around him, Dark Magic moves.

GINNY: Harry . . .

HARRY: It's fine. Go back to sleep.

GINNY: Lumos.

> *The room is filled with light from her wand. HARRY looks at her.*

> A nightmare?

HARRY: Yes.

GINNY: About what?

HARRY: The Dursleys—well, it started there—then it became something else.

> *Pause. GINNY looks at him—trying to work out where he is.*

46

GINNY: Do you want a Sleeping Draught?

HARRY: No. I'll be fine. Go back to sleep.

GINNY: You don't seem fine.

HARRY says nothing.

(Seeing his agitation.) It can't have been easy—with Amos Diggory.

HARRY: The anger I can cope with, the fact he's right is harder. Amos lost his son because of me—

GINNY: That doesn't seem particularly fair on yourself . . .

HARRY: —and there's nothing I can say—nothing I can say to anyone—unless it's the wrong thing, of course . . .

GINNY knows what—or rather who—he's referring to.

GINNY: So that's what's upsetting you? The night before Hogwarts, it's never a good night if you don't want to go. Giving Al the blanket. It was a nice try.

HARRY: It went pretty badly wrong from there. I said some things, Ginny . . .

GINNY: I heard.

HARRY: And you're still talking to me?

GINNY: Because I know that when the time is right you'll say sorry. That you didn't mean it. That what you said concealed . . . other things. You can be honest with him, Harry . . . That's all he needs.

HARRY: I just wish he was more like James or Lily.

GINNY *(dry)*: Yeah, maybe don't be that honest.

HARRY: No, I wouldn't change a thing about him . . . but I can understand them, and . . .

GINNY: Albus is different and isn't that a good thing. And he can tell, you know, when you're putting on your Harry Potter front. He wants to see the real you.

HARRY: "The truth is a beautiful and terrible thing, and should therefore be treated with great caution."

GINNY looks at him, surprised.

Dumbledore.

GINNY: A strange thing to say to a child.

HARRY: Not when you believe that child will have to die to save the world.

HARRY gasps again — and does all he can not to touch his forehead.

GINNY: Harry. What's wrong?

HARRY: Fine. I'm fine. I hear you. I'll try to be —

GINNY: Does your scar hurt?

HARRY: No. No. I'm fine. Now, Nox that and let's get some sleep.

GINNY: Harry. How long has it been since your scar hurt?

HARRY turns to GINNY, his face says it all.

HARRY: Twenty-two years.

ACT ONE, SCENE TEN

THE HOGWARTS EXPRESS

ALBUS walks quickly along the train.

ROSE: Albus, I've been looking for you . . .

ALBUS: Me? Why?

> *ROSE isn't sure how to phrase what she has to say.*

ROSE: Albus, it's the start of the fourth year, and so the start of a new year for us. I want to be friends again.

ALBUS: We never were friends.

ROSE: That's harsh! You were my best friend when I was six!

ALBUS: That was a long time ago.

> *He makes to walk away. She pulls him into an empty compartment.*

ROSE: Have you heard the rumors? Big Ministry raid a few days ago. Your dad apparently was incredibly brave.

ALBUS: How do you always know about these things and I don't?

ROSE: Apparently he—the wizard they raided—Theodore Nott, I think—had all sorts of artifacts that broke all sorts of laws including—and this has got them all gooey—an illegal Time-Turner. And quite a superior one at that.

ALBUS looks at ROSE, everything falling into place.

ALBUS: A Time-Turner? Dad found a Time-Turner?

ROSE: Shh! Yes. I know. Great, right?

ALBUS: You're sure.

ROSE: Entirely.

ALBUS: Now I have to find Scorpius.

He walks down the train. ROSE follows, still determined to say her piece.

ROSE: Albus!

ALBUS turns decisively.

ALBUS: Who's told you that you have to talk to me?

ROSE *(sprung)*: Okay, maybe your mum owled my dad—but only because she's worried about you. And I just think—

ALBUS: Leave me alone, Rose.

SCORPIUS is sitting in his usual compartment. ALBUS enters first, ROSE still tailing him.

SCORPIUS: Albus! Oh hello, Rose, what do you smell of?

ROSE: What do I *smell* of?

SCORPIUS: No, I meant it as a nice thing, you smell like a mixture of fresh flowers and fresh — bread.

ROSE: Albus, I'm here, okay? If you need me.

SCORPIUS: I mean, nice bread, good bread, bread . . . what's wrong with bread?

ROSE walks away, shaking her head.

ROSE: What's wrong with bread!

ALBUS: I've been looking for you everywhere . . .

SCORPIUS: And now you've found me. Ta-da! I was hardly hiding. You know how I like to — get on early. Stops people staring. Shouting. Writing "son of Voldemort" on my trunk. That one never gets old. She really doesn't like me, does she?

ALBUS hugs his friend. With fierceness. They hold for a beat. SCORPIUS is surprised by this.

Okay. Hello. Um. Have we hugged before? Do we hug?

The two boys awkwardly dislocate.

ALBUS: Just a slightly weird twenty-four hours.

SCORPIUS: What's happened in them?

ALBUS: I'll explain later. We have to get off this train.

There's the sound of whistles from off. The train starts moving.

SCORPIUS: Too late. The train is moving. Hogwarts ahoy!

ALBUS: Then we have to get off a moving train.

TROLLEY WITCH: Anything from the trolley, dears?

ALBUS opens a window and makes to climb out.

SCORPIUS: A moving magical train.

TROLLEY WITCH: Pumpkin Pasty? Cauldron Cake?

SCORPIUS: Albus Severus Potter, get that strange look out of your eye.

ALBUS: First question. What do you know about the Triwizard Tournament?

SCORPIUS *(happy)*: Ooooh, a quiz! Three schools pick three champions to compete in three tasks for one Cup. What's that got to do with anything?

ALBUS: You really are an enormous geek, you know that?

SCORPIUS: Ya-huh.

ALBUS: Second question. Why has the Triwizard Tournament not been run in over twenty years?

SCORPIUS: The last competition included your dad and a boy called Cedric Diggory — they decided to win together but the Cup was a Portkey — and they were transported to Voldemort. Cedric was killed. They canceled the competition immediately after.

ALBUS: Good. Third question: Did Cedric need to be killed? Easy question, easy answer: No. The words Voldemort said were "Kill the spare." The spare. He died only because he was with my father and my father couldn't save him — we can. A mistake has been made and we're going to right it. We're going to use a Time-Turner. We're going to bring him back.

SCORPIUS: Albus, for obvious reasons, I'm not a massive fan of Time-Turners . . .

ALBUS: When Amos Diggory asked for the Time-Turner my father denied they even existed. He lied to an old man who just wanted his son back—who just loved his son. And he did it because he didn't care—because he doesn't care. Everyone talks about all the brave things Dad did. But he made some mistakes too. Some big mistakes, in fact. I want to set one of those mistakes right. I want us to save Cedric.

SCORPIUS: Okay, whatever was holding your brain together seems to have snapped.

ALBUS: I'm going to do this, Scorpius. I need to do this. And you know as well as I do, I'll entirely mess it up if you don't come with me. Come on.

He grins. And then disappears ever up. SCORPIUS hesitates for a moment. He makes a face. And then hoists himself up and disappears after ALBUS.

ACT ONE, SCENE ELEVEN

ROOF OF THE HOGWARTS EXPRESS

The wind whistles from all angles and it's a fierce wind at that.

SCORPIUS: Okay, now we're on the roof of a train, it's fast, it's scary, this has been great, I feel like I've learnt a lot about me, something about you, but—

ALBUS: As I calculate it we should be approaching the viaduct soon and then it'll be a short hike to St. Oswald's Home for Old Witches and Wizards . . .

SCORPIUS: The what? The where? Look, I am as excited as you are to be a rebel for the first time in my life—yay—train roof—fun—but now—oh.

SCORPIUS sees something he doesn't want to see.

ALBUS: The water will be an extremely useful backup if our Cushioning Charm doesn't work.

SCORPIUS: Albus. The Trolley Witch.

ALBUS: You want a snack for the journey?

SCORPIUS: No. Albus. The Trolley Witch is coming towards us.

ALBUS: No, she can't be, we're on top of the train . . .

SCORPIUS points ALBUS in the right direction, and now he can see the TROLLEY WITCH, who approaches nonchalantly, pushing her trolley.

TROLLEY WITCH: Anything from the trolley, dears? Pumpkin Pasty? Chocolate Frog? Cauldron Cake?

ALBUS: Oh.

TROLLEY WITCH: People don't know much about me. They buy my Cauldron Cakes—but they never really notice me. I don't remember the last time someone asked my name.

ALBUS: What is your name?

TROLLEY WITCH: I've forgotten. All I can tell you is that when the Hogwarts Express first came to be—Ottaline Gambol herself offered me this job . . .

SCORPIUS: That's—one hundred and ninety years. You've been doing this job for one hundred and ninety years?

TROLLEY WITCH: These hands have made over six million Pumpkin Pasties. I've got quite good at them. But what people haven't noticed about my Pumpkin Pasties is how easily they transform into something else . . .

She picks up a Pumpkin Pasty. She throws it like a grenade. It explodes.

And you won't believe what I can do with my Chocolate Frogs. Never—never—have I let anyone off this train before they reached their destination. Some have tried—Sirius Black and his cronies, Fred and George Weasley. ALL HAVE FAILED.

BECAUSE THIS TRAIN—IT DOESN'T LIKE PEOPLE GETTING OFF IT . . .

The TROLLEY WITCH's hands transfigure into very sharp spikes. She smiles.

So please retake your seats for the remainder of the journey.

ALBUS: You were right, Scorpius. This train is magical.

SCORPIUS: At this precise moment in time, I take no pleasure in being right.

ALBUS: But I was also right—about the viaduct—that's water down there, time to try the Cushioning Charm.

SCORPIUS: Albus, this is a bad idea.

ALBUS: Is it? *(He has a moment's hesitation, then realizes the time for hesitation has passed.)* Too late now. Three. Two. One. Molliare!

He incants as he jumps.

SCORPIUS: Albus . . . Albus . . .

He looks down desperately after his friend. He looks at the approaching TROLLEY WITCH. Her hair wild. Her spikes particularly spiky.

Well, as fun as you clearly look, I have to go after my friend.

He pinches his nose, he jumps after ALBUS, incanting as he goes.

Molliare!

ACT ONE, SCENE TWELVE

MINISTRY OF MAGIC,
GRAND MEETING ROOM

The stage is flooded with wizards and witches. They rattle and chatter like all true wizards and witches can. Amongst them, GINNY, DRACO, and RON. Above them, on a stage, HERMIONE and HARRY.

HERMIONE: Order. Order. Do I have to conjure silence? *(She pulls silence from the crowd using her wand.)* Good. Welcome to this Extraordinary General Meeting. I'm so pleased so many of you could make it. The wizarding world has been living in peace now for many years. It's twenty-two years since we defeated Voldemort at the Battle of Hogwarts, and I'm delighted to say there is a new generation being brought up having known only the slightest conflict. Until now. Harry.

HARRY: Voldemort's allies have been showing movement for a few months now. We've followed trolls making their way across Europe, giants starting to cross the seas, and the werewolves—well, I'm distressed to say we lost sight of them some weeks ago. We don't know where they're going or who's encouraged them to move—but we are aware they are moving—and we are concerned what it might mean. So we're asking—if anyone has seen anything? Felt anything? If you could raise a wand, we will hear everyone speak. Professor McGonagall—thank you.

PROFESSOR McGONAGALL: It did look like the potions stores had been interfered with when we returned from summer break, but not a huge amount of ingredients were missing, some Boomslang skin and lacewing flies, nothing on the Restricted Register. We put it down to Peeves.

HERMIONE: Thank you, Professor. We shall investigate. *(She looks around the room.)* Nobody else? Fine, and—gravest of all—and this hasn't been the case since Voldemort—Harry's scar is hurting again.

DRACO: Voldemort is dead, Voldemort is gone.

HERMIONE: Yes, Draco, Voldemort is dead, but these things all lead us to think that there is a possibility that Voldemort—or some trace of Voldemort—might be back.

This gets a reaction.

HARRY: Now this is difficult but we have to ask it to rule it out. Those of you with a Dark Mark . . . have you felt anything? Even a twinge?

DRACO: Back to being prejudiced against those with a Dark Mark, are we, Potter?

HERMIONE: No, Draco. Harry is simply trying to—

DRACO: You know what this is about? Harry just wants his face back in the newspapers again. We've had rumors of Voldemort coming back from the *Daily Prophet* once a year every year—

HARRY: None of those rumors came from me!

DRACO: Really? Doesn't your wife edit the *Daily Prophet*?

GINNY steps towards him, outraged.

GINNY: The sports pages!

HERMIONE: Draco. Harry brought this matter to the attention of the Ministry. And I—as Minister for Magic—

DRACO: A vote you only won because you are his friend.

RON is held back by GINNY as he charges at DRACO.

RON: Do you want a smack in the mouth?

DRACO: Face it—his celebrity impacts upon you all. And how better to get everyone whispering the Potter name again than with *(he does an impression of HARRY)* "my scar is hurting, my scar is hurting." And do you know what this all means—that the gossipmongers once again have an opportunity to defame my son with these ridiculous rumors about his parentage.

HARRY: Draco, no one is saying this has anything to do with Scorpius . . .

DRACO: Well, I, for one, think this meeting a sham. And I'm leaving.

He walks out. Others start to disperse after him.

HERMIONE: No. That's not the way . . . Come back. We need a strategy.

ACT ONE, SCENE THIRTEEN

ST. OSWALD'S HOME FOR OLD WITCHES

AND WIZARDS

This is chaos. This is magic. This is St. Oswald's Home for Old Witches and Wizards and it is as wonderful as you might hope.

Walker frames are conjured into life, knitting wool is enchanted into chaos, and male nurses are made to dance tango.

These are people relieved of the burden of having to do magic for a reason—instead these witches and wizards do magic for fun. And what fun they have.

ALBUS and SCORPIUS enter, looking around themselves, amused, and let's face it, slightly scared.

ALBUS and SCORPIUS: Um, excuse me . . . Excuse me. EXCUSE ME!

SCORPIUS: Okay, so this place is wild.

ALBUS: We're looking for Amos Diggory.

> *There is suddenly total silence. Everything is instantly still. And slightly depressed.*

WOOL WOMAN: And what you boys want with that miserable old sod?

DELPHI appears with a smile.

DELPHI: Albus? Albus! You came? How wonderful! Come and say hello
to Amos!

ACT ONE, SCENE FOURTEEN

ST. OSWALD'S HOME FOR OLD WITCHES
AND WIZARDS, AMOS'S ROOM

AMOS looks at SCORPIUS and ALBUS—irritated. DELPHI watches the three of them.

AMOS: So let me get this straight. You overhear a conversation—a conversation which was not meant for you to overhear—and you decide—without prompting, in fact, without leave—to interfere, and interfere hard, in someone else's business.

ALBUS: My father lied to you—I know he did. They do have a Time-Turner.

AMOS: Of course they do. You can move along now.

ALBUS: What? No. We're here to help.

AMOS: Help? What use could a pair of undersized teenagers be for me?

ALBUS: My father proved you don't have to be grown-up to change the wizarding world.

AMOS: So I should allow you to get involved because you're a Potter? Relying on your famous name, are you?

ALBUS: No!

AMOS: A Potter who is in Slytherin House—yes, I've read about you—and who brings a Malfoy with him to visit me—a Malfoy who may be a Voldemort? Who's to say you're not involved in Dark Magic?

ALBUS: But—

AMOS: Your information was obvious but the confirmation is useful. Your father did lie. Now leave. The pair of you. And stop wasting my time.

ALBUS *(with power and strength)*: No, you need to listen to me, you said it yourself—how much blood is on my father's hands. Let me help you change that. Let me help correct one of his mistakes. Trust me.

AMOS *(his voice raised)*: Did you not hear me, boy? I see no reason to trust you. So go. Now. Before I *make* you leave.

He raises his wand ominously. ALBUS looks at the wand—he deflates— AMOS has crushed him.

SCORPIUS: Come on, mate, if there's one thing we're good at it's knowing where we're not wanted.

ALBUS is reluctant to leave. SCORPIUS pulls him by the arm. He turns and they walk away.

DELPHI: I can think of one reason why you should trust them, Uncle.

They stop.

They're the only ones volunteering to help. They're prepared to bravely put themselves at risk to return your son to your side.

In fact, I'm pretty sure they put themselves at risk even getting here . . .

AMOS: This is Cedric we're talking about . . .

DELPHI: And—didn't you say yourself, having someone inside Hogwarts might be a *massive* advantage?

DELPHI kisses the top of AMOS's head. AMOS looks at DELPHI, and then turns to look at the boys.

AMOS: Why? Why do you want to put yourself at risk? What's in it for you?

ALBUS: I know what it is to be the spare. Your son didn't deserve to be killed, Mr. Diggory. We can help you get him back.

AMOS *(finally showing emotion)*: My son—my son was the best thing that ever happened to me—and you're right, it was an injustice—a gross injustice. If you're serious . . .

ALBUS: We're deadly serious.

AMOS: This is going to be dangerous.

ALBUS: We know.

SCORPIUS: Do we?

AMOS: Delphi—perhaps if you were prepared to accompany them?

DELPHI: If that would make you happy, Uncle.

She smiles at ALBUS, he smiles back.

AMOS: You do understand even getting the Time-Turner will risk your lives.

ALBUS: We're ready to put our lives at risk.

SCORPIUS: Are we?

AMOS *(gravely)*: I hope you have it in you.

ACT ONE, SCENE FIFTEEN

HARRY AND GINNY POTTER'S HOUSE,

KITCHEN

HARRY, RON, HERMIONE, and GINNY sit, eating together.

HERMIONE: I've told Draco again and again—no one in the Ministry is saying anything about Scorpius. The rumors aren't coming from us.

GINNY: I wrote to him—after he lost Astoria—to ask if there's anything we could do. I thought maybe—as he was such a good friend to Albus—maybe Scorpius might want to stay over part of the Christmas break or . . . My owl came back with a letter containing one simple sentence: "Tell your husband to refute these allegations about my son once and for all."

HERMIONE: He's obsessed.

GINNY: He's a mess—a grieving mess.

RON: And I'm sorry for his loss but when he accuses Hermione of . . . Well . . . *(He looks across at HARRY.)* Oi droopy drawers, like I say to her all the time, it could be nothing.

HERMIONE: Her?

RON: The trolls could be going to a party, the giants to a wedding, you could be getting bad dreams because you're worried about Albus, and your scar could be hurting because you're getting old.

HARRY: Getting old? Thanks, mate.

RON: Honestly, every time I sit down now I make an "ooof" noise. An "ooof." And my feet—the trouble I'm having with my feet—I could write songs about the pain my feet give me—maybe your scar is like that.

GINNY: You talk a lot of rubbish.

RON: I consider it my speciality. That and my range of Skiving Snackboxes. And my love for all of you. Even Skinny Ginny.

GINNY: If you don't behave, Ronald Weasley, I will tell Mum.

RON: You wouldn't.

HERMIONE: If some part of Voldemort survived, in whatever form, we need to be prepared. And I'm scared.

GINNY: I'm scared too.

RON: Nothing scares me. Apart from Mum.

HERMIONE: I mean it, Harry, I will not be Cornelius Fudge on this one. I will not stick my head in the sand. And I don't care how unpopular that makes me with Draco Malfoy.

RON: You never really were one for popularity, were you?

HERMIONE shoots RON a withering look as she aims to hit him but RON jumps out of the way.

Missed.

GINNY hits RON. RON winces.

Hit. A very solid hit.

Suddenly an owl is in the room. It swoops in low and drops a letter on HARRY's plate.

HERMIONE: Bit late for an owl, isn't it?

HARRY opens the letter. Surprised.

HARRY: It's from Professor McGonagall.

GINNY: What does it say?

HARRY's face drops.

HARRY: Ginny, it's Albus—Albus and Scorpius—they never made it to school. They're missing.

ACT ONE, SCENE SIXTEEN

WHITEHALL, CELLAR

SCORPIUS is squinting at a bottle.

SCORPIUS: So we just take it?

ALBUS: Scorpius, do I really need to explain to you—übergeek and Potions expert—what Polyjuice does? Thanks to Delphi's brilliant preparation work, we are going to take this potion and be transformed, and thus disguised we will be able to enter the Ministry of Magic.

SCORPIUS: Okay, two points, one, is it painful?

DELPHI: Very—as I understand it.

SCORPIUS: Thank you. Good to know. Second point: Do either of you know what Polyjuice tastes of? Because I've heard it tastes of fish and if it does I will just vomit it back up. Fish doesn't agree with me. Never has. Never will.

DELPHI: Consider us warned. *(She knocks back the potion.)* It doesn't taste of fish. *(She begins to transform. It's agonizing.)* Actually it tastes quite pleasant, yum. It is painful but . . . *(She burps, loudly.)* Take it back.

There is a—slight—*(She burps again, she turns into HERMIONE.)* Slight—overpowering—fishy residue.

ALBUS: Okay, that's—wow.

SCORPIUS: Double wow.

DELPHI/HERMIONE: This really doesn't feel how I—I even sound like her! Triple wow.

ALBUS: Right. Me next.

SCORPIUS: No. No way, José. If we're doing this, we're doing it *(he puts on a pair of familiar-looking glasses with a smile)* together.

ALBUS: Three. Two. One.

They swallow.

No, that's good. *(He's racked with pain.)* That's less good.

They both start to transform and it's agonizing.

ALBUS turns into RON, SCORPIUS into HARRY.

The two look at each other. There's a silence.

ALBUS/RON: This is going to be slightly weird, isn't it?

SCORPIUS/HARRY *(full of drama—he's really enjoying this)*: Go to your room. Go straight to your room. You've been an incredibly awful and bad son.

ALBUS/RON *(with a laugh)*: Scorpius . . .

SCORPIUS/HARRY *(tossing his cloak over his shoulder)*: It was your idea—I be him and you be Ron! I just want to have a little fun before I . . . *(And then he burps loudly.)* Okay, so that's utterly horrible.

❧✦❧

ALBUS/RON: You know, he hides it well, but Uncle Ron's got a bit of a gut growing.

DELPHI/HERMIONE: We should go — don't you think?

They emerge onto the street. They enter a telephone box. They dial 62442.

TELEPHONE BOX: Welcome, Harry Potter. Welcome, Hermione Granger. Welcome, Ron Weasley.

They smile as the telephone box disappears into the floor.

ACT ONE, SCENE SEVENTEEN

MINISTRY OF MAGIC, MEETING ROOM

HARRY, HERMIONE, GINNY, and DRACO pace around a small room.

DRACO: Have we searched thoroughly beside the tracks . . .

HARRY: My department have searched once and are searching again.

DRACO: And the Trolley Witch is not able to tell us anything useful?

HERMIONE: The Trolley Witch is furious. She keeps talking about letting down Ottaline Gambol. She prides herself on her Hogwarts delivery record.

GINNY: Have there been any instances of magic reported by the Muggles?

HERMIONE: None so far. I have made the Muggle Prime Minister aware and he is filing what is known as a misper. Sounds like a spell. It isn't.

DRACO: So now we're relying on Muggles to find our children? Have we told them about Harry's scar too?

HERMIONE: We're merely asking the Muggles to help. And who knows how Harry's scar might be involved but it's certainly a matter

72

we're taking seriously. Our Aurors are currently investigating anyone involved in Dark Magic and —

DRACO: This is not Death Eater–related.

HERMIONE: I'm not sure I share your confidence.

DRACO: I'm not confident, I'm right. The sort of cretins pursuing Dark Magic now . . . My son is a Malfoy, they wouldn't dare.

HARRY: Unless there's something new out there, something to —

GINNY: I agree with Draco. If this is a kidnap — taking Albus I understand, taking them both . . .

HARRY locks eyes with GINNY, it becomes clear what she wants him to say.

DRACO: And Scorpius is a follower, not a leader, despite everything I've tried to instill in him. So it's undoubtedly Albus who got him from that train and my question is, where would he take him?

GINNY: Harry, they've run away, you and I know it.

DRACO notices the couple staring at each other.

DRACO: Do you? Know it? What aren't you telling us?

There's a silence.

Whatever information you're concealing, I recommend you share it now.

HARRY: Albus and I had an argument, the day before last.

DRACO: And . . .

HARRY hesitates and then makes brave eye contact with DRACO.

HARRY: And I told him that there were times when I wished he weren't my son.

There's another silence. A profoundly powerful one. And then DRACO takes a dangerous step towards HARRY.

DRACO: If anything happens to Scorpius . . .

GINNY steps in between DRACO and HARRY.

GINNY: Don't throw around threats, Draco, please don't do that.

DRACO *(roar)*: My son is missing!

GINNY *(an equal roar)*: So is mine!

He meets her look. There's real emotion in this room.

DRACO *(lip curling, every inch his father)*: If you need gold . . . Everything the Malfoys have . . . He's my sole heir . . . He's my — only family.

HERMIONE: The Ministry has plenty in reserve, thank you, Draco.

DRACO makes to leave. He stops. He looks at HARRY.

DRACO: I don't care what you did or who you saved, you are a constant curse on my family, Harry Potter.

ACT ONE, SCENE EIGHTEEN

MINISTRY OF MAGIC, CORRIDOR

SCORPIUS/HARRY: And you're sure it's in there?

A guard walks past. SCORPIUS/HARRY and DELPHI/HERMIONE try to affect performances.

Yes, Minister, I definitely think this is a matter for the Ministry to ponder at length, yes.

GUARD *(with a nod)*: Minister.

DELPHI/HERMIONE: Let's ponder it together.

He walks on, they let out a sigh of relief.

It was my uncle's idea to use the Veritaserum — we slipped it into a visiting Ministry official's drink. He told us that the Time-Turner had been kept and even told us where — the office of the Minister for Magic herself.

She indicates a door. Suddenly they hear a noise.

HERMIONE *(from off)*: Harry . . . we should talk about it . . .

HARRY *(from off)*: There's nothing to talk about.

DELPHI/HERMIONE: Oh no.

ALBUS/RON: Hermione. And Dad.

The panic is instant and infectious.

SCORPIUS/HARRY: Okay. Hiding places. No hiding places. Anyone know any Invisibility Charms?

DELPHI/HERMIONE: Do we go . . . in her office?

ALBUS/RON: She'll be coming to her office.

DELPHI/HERMIONE: There's nowhere else.

She tries the door. She tries it again.

HERMIONE *(from off)*: If you don't talk to me or Ginny about it . . .

SCORPIUS/HARRY: Stand back. Alohomora!

He aims his wand at the door. The door swings open. He grins — delighted.

Albus. Block her. It has to be you.

HARRY *(from off)*: What is there to say?

ALBUS/RON: Me. Why?

DELPHI/HERMIONE: Well, it can't be either of us, can it? We *are* them.

HERMIONE *(from off)*: What you said was obviously wrong — but — there are more factors at play here than —

ALBUS/RON: But I can't . . . I can't . . .

There's a small kerfuffle and then ALBUS/RON ends up standing outside the door as HERMIONE and HARRY enter from off.

HARRY: Hermione, I'm grateful for your concern but there's no need—

HERMIONE: Ron?

ALBUS/RON: Surprise!!!

HERMIONE: What are you doing here?

ALBUS/RON: Does a man need an excuse to see his wife?

He kisses HERMIONE firmly.

HARRY: I should go . . .

HERMIONE: Harry. My point is . . . whatever Draco says—the things you said to Albus . . . I don't think it'll do any of us any good for you to dwell on it.

ALBUS/RON: Oh, you're talking about how Harry said sometimes he wished I— *(he corrects himself)* Albus weren't his son.

HERMIONE: Ron!

ALBUS/RON: Better out than in, that's what I say . . .

HERMIONE: He'll know . . . We all say stuff we don't mean. He knows that.

ALBUS/RON: But what if sometimes we say stuff we do mean . . . What then?

HERMIONE: Ron, now's not the time, honestly.

ALBUS/RON: Of course it isn't. Bye-bye, darling.

ALBUS/RON watches her go, hopeful she'll walk past her office and away. But of course she doesn't. He runs to block her before she enters through her door. He blocks her once, and then blocks her again, swinging his hips to do so.

HERMIONE: Why are you blocking the entrance to my office?

ALBUS/RON: I'm not. Blocking. Anything.

She again makes for the door, he blocks her again.

HERMIONE: You are. Let me into my room, Ron.

ALBUS/RON: Let's have another baby.

HERMIONE tries to dodge past him.

HERMIONE: What?

ALBUS/RON: Or if not another baby, a holiday. I want a baby or a holiday and I'm going to insist on it. Shall we talk about it later, honey?

She tries to get into the room one final time, he blocks her with a kiss. It develops into quite a struggle.

Maybe with a drink in the Leaky Cauldron? Love you.

HERMIONE *(relenting)*: If there is another stink pellet in there then Merlin won't help you. Fine. We're due to update the Muggles anyway.

She exits. HARRY exits with her.

ALBUS/RON turns towards the door. She reenters, this time, alone.

A baby—OR—a holiday? Some days you are off the scale, you know that?

ALBUS/RON: It's why you married me, isn't it? My puckish sense of fun.

She exits again. He starts to open the door but again she reenters, he slams it closed.

HERMIONE: I can taste fish. I told you to stay away from those fish-
finger sandwiches.

ALBUS/RON: Right you are.

*She exits. He checks she's gone and the relief floods out of him as he opens
the door.*

ACT ONE, SCENE NINETEEN

MINISTRY OF MAGIC, HERMIONE'S OFFICE

SCORPIUS/HARRY and DELPHI/HERMIONE are waiting on the other side of HERMIONE's office door as ALBUS/RON enters — he slumps, exhausted.

ALBUS/RON: This is all too weird.

DELPHI/HERMIONE: You were impressive. Good blocking action.

SCORPIUS/HARRY: I don't know whether to high-five you or frown at you for kissing your aunt about five hundred times!

ALBUS/RON: Ron's an affectionate guy. I was trying to distract her, Scorpius. I did distract her.

SCORPIUS/HARRY: And then there's what your dad said . . .

DELPHI/HERMIONE: Boys . . . She will be back — we don't have long.

ALBUS/RON *(to SCORPIUS/HARRY):* You heard that?

DELPHI/HERMIONE: Where would Hermione hide a Time-Turner? *(She looks around the room, she sees the bookcases.)* Search the bookcases.

They start to search. SCORPIUS/HARRY looks at his friend, concerned.

SCORPIUS/HARRY: Why didn't you tell me?

ALBUS/RON: My dad says he wishes I weren't his son. Hardly a conversation starter, is it?

SCORPIUS/HARRY tries to work out what to say.

SCORPIUS/HARRY: I know the—Voldemort thing isn't—true— and—you know—but sometimes, I think I can see my dad thinking: How did I produce this?

ALBUS/RON: *Still* better than my dad. I'm pretty sure he spends most of his time thinking: How can I give him back?

DELPHI/HERMIONE tries to pull SCORPIUS/HARRY towards the bookshelves.

DELPHI/HERMIONE: Maybe if we could concentrate on the matter at hand.

SCORPIUS/HARRY: My point is, there's a reason we're friends, Albus—a reason we found each other, you know? And whatever this—adventure—is about . . .

Then he spots a book on the shelf that makes him frown.

Have you seen the books on these shelves? There are some serious books here. Banned books. Cursed books.

ALBUS/RON: How to distract Scorpius from difficult emotional issues. Take him to a library.

SCORPIUS/HARRY: All the books from the Restricted Section and then some. *Magick Moste Evile. Fifteenth-Century Fiends. Sonnets of a Sorcerer*—that's not even allowed in Hogwarts!

ALBUS/RON: *Shadows and Spirits. The Nightshade Guide to Necromancy.*

DELPHI/HERMIONE: They are quite something, aren't they . . .

ALBUS/RON: *The True History of the Opal Fire. The Imperius Curse and How to Abuse It.*

SCORPIUS/HARRY: And lookee here. Whoa. *My Eyes and How to See Past Them* by Sybill Trelawney. A book on Divination. Hermione Granger hates Divination. This is fascinating. This is a find . . .

He pulls the book from the shelf. And it falls open. And speaks.

BOOK: The first is the fourth, a disappointing mark.
You'll find it in parked but not in park.

SCORPIUS/HARRY: Okay. A book that talks. Bit weird.

BOOK: The second is the less fair of those that walk on two legs.
Grubby, hairy, a disease of the egg.
And the third is both a mountain to climb and a route to take.

ALBUS/RON: It's a riddle. It's giving us a riddle.

BOOK: A turn in the city, a glide through a lake.

DELPHI/HERMIONE: What have you done?

SCORPIUS/HARRY: I, uh, I opened a book. Something which has— in all my years on this planet—never been a particularly dangerous activity.

The books reach out and grab ALBUS. He only just eludes their grasp.

ALBUS/RON: What is that?

DELPHI/HERMIONE: She's weaponized it. She's weaponized her library. This is where the Time-Turner will be. Solve the riddle and we'll find it.

❧❖❧

ALBUS/RON: The first is the fourth. You'll find it in parked, not in park. Ed—de—

The books start to try to swallow DELPHI/HERMIONE.

SCORPIUS/HARRY: The second is a disease of the egg, the less fair of those who walk on two legs . . .

DELPHI/HERMIONE *(effusively)*: Men! De-men . . . tors. We need to find a book on dementors. *(The bookcase pulls her in.)* Albus!

ALBUS/RON: Delphi! What is going on?

SCORPIUS/HARRY: Concentrate, Albus. Do what she said. Find a book on dementors and be very careful.

ALBUS/RON: Here. *Dominating Dementors: A True History of Azkaban.*

The book flies open and swings dangerously at SCORPIUS/HARRY, who has to dodge out of the way. He falls hard against a bookcase, which attempts to consume him.

BOOK: I was born in a cage
     But smashed it with rage
     The Gaunt inside me
     Riddled me free
     Of that which would stop me to be.

ALBUS/RON: Voldemort.

DELPHI plunges through the books, back as herself.

DELPHI: Work faster!

She's pulled back in, screaming.

ALBUS/RON: Delphi! Delphi!

He tries to grab her hand, but she's gone.

SCORPIUS/HARRY: She'd become herself again — did you notice?

ALBUS/RON: No! Because I was more worried about her being eaten by a bookcase! Find. Something. Anything on him.

He finds a book.

The Heir of Slytherin? Do you think?

He pulls the book from the shelf, it pulls back, ALBUS/RON is consumed by the bookcase.

SCORPIUS/HARRY: Albus? Albus!!

But ALBUS/RON is gone.

Okay. Not that. Voldemort. Voldemort. Voldemort.

He scans the shelves.

Marvolo: The Truth, this must be . . .

He pulls it open. Again it swings away, revealing a splintering light, and a deeper voice than previously heard.

BOOK: I am the creature you have not seen.
　　I am you. I am me. The echo unforeseen.
　　Sometimes in front, sometimes behind,
　　A constant companion, for we are entwined.

ALBUS emerges from the books. As himself again.

SCORPIUS/HARRY: Albus . . .

He tries to grab him.

ALBUS: No. Just — THIIIIIIINK.

ALBUS is violently pulled back into the bookcase.

SCORPIUS/HARRY: But I can't . . . an invisible echo, what is that? The only thing I'm good at is thinking and when I need to think — I can't.

The books pull him inside them; he's powerless. This is terrifying.

There's silence.

Then BANG — a shower of books are released from the bookcase — and SCORPIUS reemerges. Smashing the books aside.

SCORPIUS: No! You don't! Sybill Trelawney. No!!!!

He looks around, sunk but full of energy.

This is all wrong. Albus? Can you hear me? All this for a frigging Time-Turner. Think, Scorpius. Think.

Books try and grab him.

A constant companion. Sometimes behind. Sometimes in front. Hang on. I've missed it. Shadow. You're a shadow. *Shadows and Spirits.* It must be . . .

He climbs up the bookcase, which is horrifying as it rises up at him. Grabbing at him with his every step.

He pulls the book from the shelf. It comes out and the noise and chaos suddenly stop.

Is that —

Suddenly there's a smashing and ALBUS and DELPHI fall out of the shelves and down to the floor.

We beat it. We beat the library.

ALBUS: Delphi, are you . . . ?

DELPHI: Wow. Quite a ride.

ALBUS notices the book SCORPIUS is holding to his chest.

ALBUS: Is that? Scorpius? What's inside that book?

DELPHI: I think we should find out, don't you?

SCORPIUS opens the book. In the center of it—a spinning Time-Turner.

SCORPIUS: We've found the Time-Turner—I never thought we'd get this far.

ALBUS: Mate, now we've got this, the next stop is saving Cedric. Our journey has only just begun.

SCORPIUS: Only just begun and it's almost half killed us. Good. This is going to be good.

Whispers rise to a roar. And we cut to black.

ACT TWO

ACT TWO, SCENE ONE

⁂

DREAM, PRIVET DRIVE,
CUPBOARD UNDER THE STAIRS

AUNT PETUNIA: Harry. Harry. These pots aren't clean. **THESE POTS ARE A DISGRACE. HARRY POTTER.** Wake up.

YOUNG HARRY wakes to see AUNT PETUNIA bearing down on him.

YOUNG HARRY: Aunt Petunia. What time is it?

AUNT PETUNIA: Time enough. You know, when we agreed to take you in, we hoped we could improve you — build you — make you a decent human being. So I suppose it's only ourselves we've got to blame that you've turned out . . . such a limp disappointment.

YOUNG HARRY: I try —

AUNT PETUNIA: Trying is not succeeding though, is it? There are grease smears on the glasses. There are scuff marks on the pots. Now get up and go to the kitchen and get scrubbing.

He gets out of bed. There's a wet smear down the back of his trousers.

Oh no. Oh no. What have you done? You've wet the bed, again.

❧❖❧

She pulls back the covers.

This is very unacceptable.

YOUNG HARRY: I'm — sorry, I think I was having a nightmare.

AUNT PETUNIA: You disgusting boy. Only animals wet themselves. Animals and disgusting little boys.

YOUNG HARRY: It was about my mum and dad. I think I saw them — I think I saw them — die?

AUNT PETUNIA: And why would I have the slightest bit of interest in that?

YOUNG HARRY: There was a man shouting Adkava Ad-something Acabra — Ad — and the noise of a snake hissing. I could hear my mum scream.

AUNT PETUNIA takes a moment to reset herself.

AUNT PETUNIA: If you were really reliving their death, all you'd hear would be a screech of brakes and a horrific thud. Your parents died in a car accident. You know that. I don't think your mother had even time to scream. Lord spare you the details more than that. Now strip those sheets, get in the kitchen, and get scrubbing. I don't want to have to tell you again.

She exits with a bang.

And YOUNG HARRY is left holding the sheets.

And the stage contorts and trees rise as the dream twists into something else entirely.

Suddenly, ALBUS appears and stands looking at YOUNG HARRY.

PART ONE

❧❀❧

And then, right from the back of the room, Parseltongue whispers around everyone.

He's coming. He's coming.

Words said in an unmistakable voice. The voice of VOLDEMORT . . .

Haaarry Pottttter.

ACT TWO, SCENE TWO

HARRY AND GINNY POTTER'S HOUSE,

STAIRCASE

HARRY wakes in the darkness, breathing deeply. His exhaustion palpable, his fear overwhelming.

HARRY: Lumos.

GINNY enters, surprised by the light.

GINNY: Okay . . . ?

HARRY: I was sleeping.

GINNY: You were.

HARRY: You weren't. Any — news? Any owls or . . . ?

GINNY: None.

HARRY: I was dreaming — I was under the stairs and then I — I heard him — Voldemort — so clearly.

GINNY: Voldemort?

HARRY: And then I saw—Albus. In red—he was wearing Durmstrang robes.

GINNY: Durmstrang robes?

HARRY thinks.

HARRY: Ginny, I think I know where he is . . .

ACT TWO, SCENE THREE

HOGWARTS, HEADMISTRESS'S OFFICE

HARRY and GINNY stand in PROFESSOR McGONAGALL's office.

PROFESSOR McGONAGALL: And we don't know where in the Forbidden Forest?

HARRY: I haven't had a dream like it for years. But Albus was there. I know he was.

GINNY: We need to get searching as quickly as possible.

PROFESSOR McGONAGALL: I can give you Professor Longbottom — his knowledge of plants might be useful — and —

Suddenly there is a rumble in the chimney. PROFESSOR McGONAGALL looks at it, concerned. Then HERMIONE tumbles out.

HERMIONE: Is it true? Can I help?

PROFESSOR McGONAGALL: Minister — this is quite unexpected . . .

GINNY: That may be my fault — I persuaded them to put out an emergency edition of the *Daily Prophet*. Asking for volunteers.

PROFESSOR McGONAGALL: Right. Very sensible. I expect . . . there will be quite a few.

RON bursts in. Covered in soot. Wearing a gravy-stained dinner napkin.

RON: Have I missed anything—I couldn't work out which Floo to travel to. Ended up in the kitchen somehow. *(HERMIONE glares as he pulls the napkin off himself.)* What?

Suddenly there is another rumble in the chimney and DRACO comes down hard, surrounded by cascading soot and dust.

Everyone looks at him, surprised. He stands and brushes the soot off himself.

DRACO: Sorry about your floor, Minerva.

PROFESSOR McGONAGALL: I dare say it's my fault for owning a chimney.

HARRY: Quite a surprise to see you, Draco. I thought you didn't believe in my dreams.

DRACO: I don't, but I do trust your luck. Harry Potter is always where the action is at. And I need my son back with me and safe.

GINNY: Then let's get to the Forbidden Forest and find them both.

ACT TWO, SCENE FOUR

EDGE OF THE FORBIDDEN FOREST

ALBUS and DELPHI face each other, holding wands.

ALBUS: Expelliarmus!

DELPHI's wand flies through the air.

DELPHI: You're getting it now. You're good at this.

She takes her wand back from him.

(In a posh voice.) "You're a positively disarming young man."

ALBUS: Expelliarmus!

Her wand flies back again.

DELPHI: And we have a winner.

The two high-five.

ALBUS: I've never been good at spells.

SCORPIUS appears at the back of the stage. He looks at his friend talking to a girl—and part of him likes it and part of him doesn't.

DELPHI: I was rubbish—and then something clicked. And it will for you too. Not that I'm a super witch or anything but— I think you're becoming quite some wizard, Albus Potter.

ALBUS: Then you should stick around, teach me more . . .

DELPHI: Of course I'm sticking around, we're friends, aren't we?

ALBUS: Yes. Yes. Definitely friends. Definitely.

DELPHI: Great. Wizzo!

SCORPIUS: What's wizzo?

SCORPIUS steps forward decisively.

ALBUS: Cracked the spell. I mean, it's pretty basic, but I was—well, I cracked it.

SCORPIUS *(over-enthusiastic, trying to join in)*: And I've found our way through to the school. Listen, are we sure this will work . . .

DELPHI: Yes!

ALBUS: It's a brilliant plan. The secret to not getting Cedric killed is to stop him winning the Triwizard Tournament. If he doesn't win, he can't be killed.

SCORPIUS: And I understand that, but . . .

ALBUS: So we just need to mess up his chances supremely badly in task one. The first task is getting a golden egg from a dragon, how did Cedric distract the dragon—

DELPHI puts her hand in the air. ALBUS grins and points at her. These two are getting on really well now.

Diggory.

DELPHI:—by transfiguring a stone into a dog.

ALBUS:—well, a little Expelliarmus and he won't be able to do that.

SCORPIUS isn't enjoying the DELPHI-ALBUS double act.

SCORPIUS: Okay, two points, first point, we're certain the dragon won't kill him?

DELPHI: It's always two points with him, isn't it? Of course it won't. This is Hogwarts. They won't let damage happen to any of the champions.

SCORPIUS: Okay, second *point*—more significant *point*—we're going back without any knowledge of whether we can travel back afterwards. Which is exciting. Maybe we should just—try going back an hour, say, first and then . . .

DELPHI: I'm sorry, Scorpius, we've no time to waste. Waiting here this close to the school is just too dangerous—I'm sure they'll be looking for you and . . .

ALBUS: She's right.

DELPHI: Now, you're going to need to wear these.

She pulls out two large paper bags. The boys pull robes from them.

ALBUS: But these are Durmstrang robes.

DELPHI: My uncle's idea. If you are in Hogwarts robes people will expect to know who you are. But there are two other schools competing at the Triwizard Tournament—and if you're in Durmstrang robes—well, you can fade into the background, can't you?

ALBUS: Good thinking! Hang on, where are your robes?

DELPHI: Albus, I'm flattered, but I don't think I can pretend to be a student, do you? I'll just keep in the background and pretend to be a—ooh, maybe I could pretend to be a dragon tamer. You're doing all the spell stuff anyway.

SCORPIUS looks at her and then at ALBUS.

SCORPIUS: You shouldn't come.

DELPHI: What?

SCORPIUS: You're right. We don't need you for the spell. And if you can't wear student robes—you're too big a risk. Sorry, Delphi, you shouldn't come.

DELPHI: But I have to—he's my cousin. Albus?

ALBUS: I think he's right. I'm sorry.

DELPHI: What?

ALBUS: We won't mess up.

DELPHI: But without me—you won't be able to work the Time-Turner.

SCORPIUS: You taught us how to use the Time-Turner.

DELPHI is really upset.

DELPHI: No. I won't let you do this . . .

ALBUS: You told your uncle to trust us. Now it's your turn. The school is close now. We should leave you here.

DELPHI looks at them both and takes a deep breath. She nods to herself and smiles.

DELPHI: Then go. But — just know this . . . Today you get an opportunity few are given — today you get to change history — to change time itself. But more than all that, today you get the chance to give an old man his son back.

She smiles. She looks at ALBUS. She leans down and gently kisses him on both cheeks.

She walks away into the woodland. ALBUS stares after her.

SCORPIUS: She didn't kiss me — did you notice? *(He looks at his friend.)* Are you okay, Albus? You look a little pale. And red. Pale and red at the same time.

ALBUS: Let's do this.

ACT TWO, SCENE FIVE

FORBIDDEN FOREST

The forest seems to grow bigger, thicker—and amongst the trees, people searching, looking for the missing wizards. But slowly people melt away until HARRY is left alone.

He hears something. He turns to his right.

HARRY: Albus? Scorpius? Albus?

> *And then he hears the sound of hooves. HARRY is startled. He looks around for where the noise is coming from.*
>
> *Suddenly BANE steps forward into the light. He is a magnificent centaur.*

BANE: Harry Potter.

HARRY: Good. You still recognize me, Bane.

BANE: You've grown older.

HARRY: I have.

BANE: But not wiser. For you trespass on our land.

HARRY: I have always respected the centaurs. We are not enemies. You fought bravely at the Battle of Hogwarts. And I fought beside you.

BANE: I did my part. But for my herd, and our honor. Not for you. And after the battle, the forest was deemed centaur land. And if you're on our land — without permission — then you are our enemy.

HARRY: My son is missing, Bane. I need help finding him.

BANE: And he is here? In our forest?

HARRY: Yes.

BANE: Then he is as stupid as you are.

HARRY: Can you help me, Bane?

There's a pause. BANE looks down at HARRY imperiously.

BANE: I can only tell you what I know . . . But I tell you not for your benefit but for the benefit of my herd. The centaurs do not need another war.

HARRY: Neither do we! What do you know?

BANE: I've seen your son, Harry Potter. Seen him in the movements of the stars.

HARRY: You've seen him in the stars?

BANE: I can't tell you where he is. I can't tell you how you'll find him.

HARRY: But you've seen something? You've divined something?

BANE: There is a black cloud around your son, a dangerous black cloud.

HARRY: Around Albus?

BANE: A black cloud that may endanger us all. You'll find your son again, Harry Potter. But then you could lose him forever.

He makes a sound like a horse's cry — and then makes hard away — leaving a bewildered HARRY behind. He begins to search again — now with even more fervor.

HARRY: Albus! Albus!

ACT TWO, SCENE SIX

EDGE OF THE FORBIDDEN FOREST

SCORPIUS and ALBUS round a corner to be faced with a gap in the trees . . .

A gap through which is visible . . . a glorious light . . .

SCORPIUS: And there it is . . .

ALBUS: Hogwarts. Never seen this view of it before.

SCORPIUS: Still get a tingle, don't you? When you see it?

> *And revealed through the trees is HOGWARTS — a splendid mass of bulbous buildings and towers.*

> From the moment I first heard of it, I was desperate to go. I mean, Dad didn't much like it there but even the way he described it . . . From the age of ten I'd check the *Daily Prophet* first thing every morning — certain some sort of tragedy would have befallen it — certain I wouldn't get to go.

ALBUS: And then you got there and it turned out to be terrible after all.

SCORPIUS: Not for me.

> *ALBUS looks at his friend, shocked.*

All I ever wanted to do was go to Hogwarts and have a mate to get up to mayhem with. Just like Harry Potter. And I got his son. How crazily fortunate is that.

ALBUS: But I'm nothing like my dad.

SCORPIUS: You're better. You're my best friend, Albus. And this is mayhem to the nth degree. Which is great, thumbs-up great, it's just—I have got to say—I don't mind admitting—I am a tiny bit—just a tiny bit scared.

ALBUS looks at SCORPIUS and smiles.

ALBUS: You're my best friend too. And don't worry—I have a good feeling about this.

We hear RON's voice from off—he's clearly in close proximity.

RON: Albus? Albus.

ALBUS turns towards it, scared.

ALBUS: But we've got to go—now.

ALBUS takes the Time-Turner from SCORPIUS—he presses down upon it and the Time-Turner begins to vibrate and then explodes into a storm of movement.

And with it the stage starts to transform. The two boys look at it.

And there is a giant whoosh of light. A smash of noise.

And time stops. And then it turns over, thinks a bit, and begins spooling backwards, slow at first . . .

And then it speeds up.

ACT TWO, SCENE SEVEN

TRIWIZARD TOURNAMENT,
EDGE OF THE FORBIDDEN FOREST, 1994

Suddenly everything is a riot of noise as a crowd consumes ALBUS and SCORPIUS.

And suddenly the "greatest showman on earth" (his words, not ours) is onstage, using Sonorus to amplify his voice, and . . . well . . . he's having a ball.

LUDO BAGMAN: Ladies and gentlemen—boys and girls—I give you—the greatest—the fabulous—the one—and the only TRIWIZARD TOURNAMENT.

There's a loud cheer.

If you're from Hogwarts. Give me a cheer.

There's a loud cheer.

If you're from Durmstrang—give me a cheer.

There's a loud cheer.

AND IF YOU'RE FROM BEAUXBATONS GIVE ME A CHEER.

There's a slightly limp cheer.

⚛️

Slightly less enthusiastic from the French there.

SCORPIUS *(smiling)*: This has worked. That's Ludo Bagman.

LUDO BAGMAN: And there they are. Ladies and gentlemen — boys and girls — I present to you — the reason why we're all here — THE CHAMPIONS. Representing Durmstrang, what eyebrows, what a gait, what a boy, there's nothing he won't try on a broomstick, it's Viktor Krazy Krum.

SCORPIUS and ALBUS *(who are really getting into playing the Durmstrang students now)*: Go, go, Krazy Krum. Go, go, Krazy Krum.

LUDO BAGMAN: From the Beauxbatons Academy — *zut alors*, it's Fleur Delacour!

There's some polite applause.

And from Hogwarts not one but two students, he makes us all go weaky at the kneesy, he's Cedric Delicious Diggory.

The crowd go wild.

And then the other — you know him as the Boy Who Lived, I know him as the boy who keeps surprising us all . . .

ALBUS: That's my dad.

LUDO BAGMAN: Yes, it's Harry Plucky Potter.

There's cheering. Particularly from a nervous-looking girl at the edge of the crowd — this is YOUNG HERMIONE (played by the same actress as plays ROSE). It is noticeable that the cheering for HARRY is slightly less than that for CEDRIC.

And now—silence please, all. The—first—task. Retrieving a golden egg. From a nest of—ladies and gentlemen, boys and girls, I give you—DRAGONS. And guiding the dragons— CHARLIE WEASLEY.

There are more cheers.

YOUNG HERMIONE: If you're going to stand so close I'd rather you didn't breathe on me quite so much.

SCORPIUS: Rose? What are you doing here?

YOUNG HERMIONE: Who's Rose? And what's happened to your accent?

ALBUS *(with a bad accent)*: Sorry. Hermione. He's got you mixed up with someone else.

YOUNG HERMIONE: How do you know my name?

LUDO BAGMAN: And with no time to lose let's bring out our first champion—facing a Swedish Short-Snout, I give you— CEDRIC DIGGORY.

A dragon roar distracts YOUNG HERMIONE, and ALBUS readies his wand.

And Cedric Diggory has entered the stage. And he seems ready. Scared, but ready. He dodges this way. He dodges that. The girls swoon as he dives for cover. They cry as one: Don't damage our Diggory, Mr. Dragon!

SCORPIUS looks concerned.

SCORPIUS: Albus, something is going wrong. The Time-Turner, it's shaking.

A ticking begins, an incessant, dangerous ticking. It's coming from the Time-Turner.

LUDO BAGMAN: And Cedric skirts left and he dives right — and he readies his wand — what has this young, brave, handsome man got up his sleevies now —

ALBUS *(extending his wand)*: Expelliarmus!

CEDRIC's wand is summoned to ALBUS's hand.

LUDO BAGMAN: — but no, what's this? Is it Dark Magic or is it something else entirely? His wand is flying away — Cedric Diggory is Disarmed —

SCORPIUS: Albus, I think the Time-Turner — something is wrong . . .

The Time-Turner's ticking gets louder still.

LUDO BAGMAN: It's all going wrong for Diggors. This could be the end of the task for him. The end of the tournament.

SCORPIUS grabs ALBUS.

There's a crescendo in the ticking, and a flash.

And time is turned back to the present, with ALBUS hollering in pain.

SCORPIUS: Albus! Did it hurt you? Albus, are you —

ALBUS: What happened?

SCORPIUS: There must be some limit — the Time-Turner must have some kind of *time* limit . . .

ALBUS: Do you think we've done it? Do you think we've changed anything?

Suddenly the stage is invaded from all sides by HARRY, RON (who now has a side parting in his hair and whose wardrobe choices have become rather more staid), GINNY, and DRACO. SCORPIUS looks at them all — and slips the Time-Turner back into his pocket. ALBUS looks at them rather more blankly — he's in a lot of pain.

RON: I told you. I told you I saw them.

SCORPIUS: I think we're about to find out.

ALBUS: Hello, Dad. Is something wrong?

HARRY looks at his son disbelievingly.

HARRY: Yes. You could say that.

ALBUS collapses onto the floor. HARRY and GINNY rush to help.

ACT TWO, SCENE EIGHT

◄◆►

HOGWARTS, HOSPITAL WING

ALBUS is asleep in a hospital bed. HARRY sits troubled beside him. Above them is a picture of a concerned kindly man. HARRY rubs his eyes — stands — and walks around the room. He stretches out his back.

And then he meets eyes with the painting. Which looks startled to be spotted. And HARRY looks startled back.

HARRY: Professor Dumbledore.

DUMBLEDORE: Good evening, Harry.

HARRY: I've missed you. Whenever I've dropped in on the headmistress lately, your frame's been empty.

DUMBLEDORE: Ah, well, I do like to pop into my other portraits now and then. *(He looks at ALBUS.)* Will he be all right?

HARRY: He's been out twenty-four hours, mostly in order so Madam Pomfrey could reset his arm. She said it was the strangest thing, it's like it was broken twenty years ago and allowed to set in the "most contrary" of directions. She says he'll be fine.

DUMBLEDORE: A difficult thing, I imagine, to watch your child in pain.

HARRY looks up at DUMBLEDORE, and then down at ALBUS.

HARRY: I've never asked how you felt about me naming him after you, have I?

DUMBLEDORE: Candidly, Harry, it seemed a great weight to place upon the poor boy.

HARRY: I need your help. I need your advice. Bane says Albus is in danger. How do I protect my son, Dumbledore?

DUMBLEDORE: You ask me, of all people, how to protect a boy in terrible danger? We cannot protect the young from harm. Pain must and will come.

HARRY: So I'm supposed to stand and watch?

DUMBLEDORE: No. You're supposed to teach him how to meet life.

HARRY: How? He won't listen.

DUMBLEDORE: Perhaps he's waiting for you to see him clearly.

HARRY frowns as he tries to digest this.

(*With sensitivity.*) It is a portrait's curse and blessing to . . . hear things. At the school, at the Ministry, I hear people talking . . .

HARRY: And what is the gossip about me and my son?

DUMBLEDORE: Not gossip. Concern. That you two are struggling. That he's difficult. That he is angry with you. I have formed the impression that — perhaps — you are blinded by your love for him.

HARRY: Blinded?

DUMBLEDORE: You must see him as he is, Harry. You must look for what's wounding him.

HARRY: Haven't I seen him as he is? What's wounding my son? *(He thinks.)* Or is it who's wounding my son?

ALBUS *(mumbles in his sleep)*: Dad . . .

HARRY: This black cloud, it's someone, isn't it? Not something?

DUMBLEDORE: Ah really, what does my opinion matter anymore? I am paint and memory, Harry, paint and memory. And I never had a son.

HARRY: But I need your advice.

ALBUS: Dad?

HARRY looks at ALBUS and then back at DUMBLEDORE. But DUMBLEDORE is gone.

HARRY: No, where have you gone now?

ALBUS: We're in — the hospital wing?

HARRY turns his attention back to ALBUS.

HARRY *(discombobulated)*: Yes. And you're — you will be fine. For recuperation, Madam Pomfrey wasn't sure what to prescribe and said you should probably eat lots of — chocolate. Actually, do you mind if I have some — ? I've got something to tell you and I don't think you'll like it.

ALBUS looks at his dad, what does he have to say? He decides not to engage.

ALBUS: Okay. I think.

HARRY takes some chocolate, he eats a big chunk. ALBUS looks at his dad, confused.

Better?

HARRY: Much.

He holds out the chocolate to his son. ALBUS takes a piece. Father and son munch together.

The arm, how does it feel?

ALBUS flexes his arm.

ALBUS: It feels great.

HARRY *(soft)*: Where did you go, Albus? I can't tell you what it did to us. Your mum was worried sick . . .

ALBUS looks up, he is a great liar.

ALBUS: We decided we didn't want to come to school. We thought we could start again—in the Muggle world. We discovered we were wrong. We were coming back to Hogwarts when you found us.

HARRY: In Durmstrang robes?

ALBUS: The robes were . . . The whole thing—Scorpius and I—we didn't think.

HARRY: And why—why did you run? Because of me? Because of what I said?

ALBUS: I don't know. Hogwarts isn't actually that pleasant a place when you don't fit in.

HARRY: And did Scorpius—encourage you to—go?

ALBUS: Scorpius? No.

HARRY looks at ALBUS, trying to see almost an aura around him, thinking deeply.

HARRY: I need you to stay away from Scorpius Malfoy.

ALBUS: What? Scorpius?

HARRY: I don't know how you became friends in the first place, but you did, and now — I need you to —

ALBUS: My best friend? My only friend?

HARRY: He's dangerous.

ALBUS: Scorpius? Dangerous? Have you met him? Dad, if you honestly think he's the son of Voldemort . . .

HARRY: I don't know what he is, I just know you need to stay away from him. Bane told me —

ALBUS: Who's Bane?

HARRY: A centaur with profound Divination skills. He said there's a black cloud around you and —

ALBUS: A black cloud?

HARRY: And I have very good reason to believe that Dark Magic is in a resurgence and I need to keep you safe from it. Safe from him. Safe from Scorpius.

ALBUS hesitates a moment, and then his face strengthens.

ALBUS: And if I won't? Stay away from him?

HARRY looks at his son, thinking quickly.

HARRY: There's a map. It used to be used for those wanting to get up to no good. Now we're going to use it to keep an eye — a permanent eye — on you. Professor McGonagall will watch your every movement. Any time you are seen together — she'll come flying — any time you attempt to leave Hogwarts — she'll fly. I expect you to go to your lessons — none of which you will now share with Scorpius, and between times, you will stay in the Gryffindor common room!

ALBUS: You can't make me go into Gryffindor! I'm Slytherin!

HARRY: Don't play games, Albus, you know what House you are. If she finds you with Scorpius, I will fix you with a spell which will allow me eyes and ears into your every movement, your every conversation. In the meantime, investigations will begin in my department as to his true heritage.

ALBUS *(starting to cry)*: But, Dad — you can't — that's just not . . .

HARRY: I thought for a long time I wasn't a good enough dad for you because you didn't like me. It's only now I realize that I don't need you to like me, I need you to obey me because I'm your dad and I do know better. I'm sorry, Albus. It has to be this way.

ACT TWO, SCENE NINE

HOGWARTS, STAIRCASE

ALBUS pursues HARRY across the stage.

ALBUS: What if I run? I'll run.

HARRY: Albus, get back in bed.

ALBUS: I'll run away again.

HARRY: No. You won't.

ALBUS: I will — and this time I'll make sure Ron can't find us.

RON: Do I hear my name?

> *RON enters on a staircase, his side parting now super-aggressive, his robes just a little bit too short, his clothes now spectacularly staid.*

ALBUS: Uncle Ron! Thank Dumbledore. If ever we needed one of your jokes it's now . . .

> *RON frowns, confused.*

RON: Jokes? I don't know any jokes.

ALBUS: Of course you do. You run a joke shop.

RON *(now supremely confused)*: A joke shop? Well now. Anyway I'm pleased I caught you. I was going to bring some sweets — for a, uh, sort of, a, get well soon, but, uh . . . Actually Padma — she thinks about things a lot more — deeply — than I do — and she thought it'd be nicer for you to get something useful for school. So we got you a — set of quills. Yes. Yes. Yes. Look at these bad boys. Top of the range.

ALBUS: Who's Padma?

HARRY frowns at ALBUS.

HARRY: Your aunt.

ALBUS: I have an Aunt Padma?

RON *(to HARRY)*: Taken a Confundus Charm to the head, has he? *(To ALBUS.)* My wife, Padma. You remember. Talks slightly too close to your face, smells a bit minty. *(Leans in.)* Padma, mother of Panju! *(To HARRY.)* That's why I'm here, of course. Panju. He's in trouble again. I wanted to just send a Howler but Padma insisted I come in person. I don't know why. He just laughs at me.

ALBUS: But . . . you're married to Hermione.

Beat. RON doesn't understand this at all.

RON: Hermione. No. Nooooo. Merlin's beard.

HARRY: Albus has also forgotten that he was sorted into Gryffindor. Conveniently.

RON: Yes, well, sorry, old chap, but you're a Gryffindor.

ALBUS: But how did I get sorted into Gryffindor?

RON: You persuaded the Sorting Hat, don't you remember? Panju bet you that you couldn't get into Gryffindor if your life depended on it, so you chose Gryffindor to spite him. I can't blame you, *(dry)* we'd all like to wipe the smile off his face sometimes, wouldn't we? *(Terrified.)* Please don't tell Padma I said that.

ALBUS: Who's Panju?

RON and HARRY stare at ALBUS.

RON: Bloody hell, you're really not yourself, are you? Anyway, better go, before I'm sent a Howler myself.

He stumbles on, not even an inch of the man he was.

ALBUS: But that doesn't . . . make sense.

HARRY: Albus, whatever you're feigning, it isn't working. I will not change my mind.

ALBUS: Dad, you have two choices, either you take me to —

HARRY: No, you're the one with the choice, Albus. You do this, or you get in deeper, much deeper trouble — do you understand?

SCORPIUS: Albus? You're okay. That's fantastic.

HARRY: He's completely cured. And we've got to go.

ALBUS looks up at SCORPIUS and his heart breaks. He walks on.

SCORPIUS: Are you mad at me? What's going on?

ALBUS stops and turns to SCORPIUS.

ALBUS: Did it work? Did any of it work?

SCORPIUS: No . . . But, Albus —

HARRY: Albus. Whatever gibberish you're talking, you need to stop it, now. This is your final warning.

ALBUS looks torn between his dad and his friend.

ALBUS: I can't, okay?

SCORPIUS: You can't what?

ALBUS: Just—we'll be better off without each other, okay?

SCORPIUS is left looking up after him. Heartbroken.

ACT TWO, SCENE TEN

HOGWARTS, HEADMISTRESS'S OFFICE

PROFESSOR McGONAGALL is full of unhappiness, HARRY is full of purpose, GINNY is not sure what she's supposed to be.

PROFESSOR McGONAGALL: I'm not sure this is what the Marauder's Map was intended for.

HARRY: If you see them together, then get to them as quickly as possible, and keep them separate.

PROFESSOR McGONAGALL: Harry, are you sure this is the right decision? Because far be it from me to doubt the wisdom of the centaurs, but Bane is an extremely angry centaur and . . . it's not beyond him to twist the constellations for his own ends.

HARRY: I trust Bane. Albus is to stay away from Scorpius. For his sake, and others.

GINNY: I think what Harry means is . . .

HARRY *(with finality)*: The professor knows what I mean.

GINNY looks at HARRY, surprised that he'd talk to her that way.

PROFESSOR McGONAGALL: Albus has been checked by the greatest witches and wizards in the country and no one can find or sense a hex or a curse.

HARRY: And Dumbledore — Dumbledore said —

PROFESSOR McGONAGALL: What?

HARRY: His portrait. We spoke. He said some things which made sense —

PROFESSOR McGONAGALL: Dumbledore is dead, Harry. And I've told you before, portraits don't represent even half of their subjects.

HARRY: He said love had blinded me.

PROFESSOR McGONAGALL: A head teacher's portrait is a memoir. It is supposed to be a support mechanism for the decisions I have to make. But I was advised as I took this job to not mistake the painting for the person. And you would be well-advised to do the same.

HARRY: But he was right. I see it now.

PROFESSOR McGONAGALL: Harry, you've been put under enormous pressure, the loss of Albus, the search for him, the fears as to what your scar might mean. But trust me when I tell you, you are making a mistake.

HARRY: Albus didn't like me before. He might not like me again. But he will be safe. With the greatest respect, Minerva — you don't have children —

GINNY: Harry!

HARRY: — you don't understand.

PROFESSOR McGONAGALL *(deeply hurt)*: I'd hope that a lifetime spent in the teaching profession would mean . . .

HARRY: This map will reveal to you where my son is at all times—I expect you to use it. And if I hear you don't—then I will come down on this school as hard as I can—using the full force of the Ministry—is that understood?

PROFESSOR McGONAGALL *(bewildered by this vitriol)*: Perfectly.

GINNY looks at HARRY, unsure of what he's become. He doesn't look back.

ACT TWO, SCENE ELEVEN

HOGWARTS, DEFENSE AGAINST
THE DARK ARTS CLASSROOM

ALBUS enters the classroom—slightly unsure.

HERMIONE: Ah yes. Our train absconder. Finally joining us.

ALBUS: Hermione?

He looks amazed. HERMIONE is standing at the front of the lesson.

HERMIONE: Professor Granger I believe is my name, Potter.

ALBUS: What are you doing here?

HERMIONE: Teaching. For my sins. What are you doing here? Learning, I hope.

ALBUS: But you're . . . you're . . . Minister for Magic.

HERMIONE: Been having those dreams again, have you, Potter? Today we're going to look at Patronus Charms.

ALBUS *(amazed)*: You're our Defense Against the Dark Arts teacher?

There are titters.

HERMIONE: Losing patience now. Ten points from Gryffindor for stupidity.

POLLY CHAPMAN *(standing, full of affront)*: No. No. He's doing it deliberately. He hates Gryffindor and everyone knows it.

HERMIONE: Sit down, Polly Chapman, before this gets even worse. *(POLLY sighs and then sits.)* And I suggest you join her, Albus. And end this charade.

ALBUS: But you're not this mean.

HERMIONE: And that's twenty points from Gryffindor to assure Albus Potter that I am this mean.

YANN FREDERICKS: If you don't sit down right now, Albus . . .

ALBUS sits.

ALBUS: Can I just say —

HERMIONE: No, you can't. Just keep quiet, Potter, otherwise you'll lose what limited popularity you already have. Now who can tell me what a Patronus is? No? No one. You really are a most disappointing bunch.

HERMIONE smiles a thin smile. She really is quite mean.

ALBUS: No. This is stupid. Where's Rose? She'll tell you that you're being ridiculous.

HERMIONE: Who's Rose? Your invisible friend?

ALBUS: Rose Granger-Weasley! Your daughter! *(He realizes.)* Of course — because you and Ron aren't married Rose —

There's giggling.

HERMIONE: How dare you! Fifty points from Gryffindor. And I assure you if anyone interrupts me again it'll be a hundred points . . .

She stares around the room. No one moves a muscle.

Good. A Patronus is a magical charm, a projection of all your most positive feelings, and takes the shape of the animal with whom you share the deepest affinity. It is a gift of light. If you can conjure a Patronus, you can protect yourself against the world. Which, in some of our cases, seems like a necessity sooner rather than later.

ACT TWO, SCENE TWELVE

HOGWARTS, STAIRCASES

ALBUS walks up a staircase. Looking around as he does.

He doesn't see anything. He exits. The staircases move in almost a dance.

SCORPIUS enters behind him. He thinks he's seen ALBUS, he realizes he isn't there.

He slumps down to the floor as the staircase sweeps around.

MADAM HOOCH enters and walks up the staircase. At the top, she gestures for SCORPIUS to move.

He does. And slopes off — his abject loneliness clear.

ALBUS enters and walks up one staircase.

SCORPIUS enters and walks up another.

The staircases meet. The two boys look at each other.

Lost and hopeful — all at once.

And then ALBUS looks away and the moment is broken — and with it, possibly, the friendship.

And now the staircases part — the two look at each other — one full of guilt — the other full of pain — both full of unhappiness.

ACT TWO, SCENE THIRTEEN

HARRY AND GINNY POTTER'S HOUSE, KITCHEN

GINNY and HARRY watch each other warily. There is an argument due, and both of them know it.

HARRY: This is the right decision.

GINNY: You almost sound convinced.

HARRY: You told me to be honest with him, but actually I needed to be honest with myself, trust what my heart was telling me . . .

GINNY: Harry, you have one of the greatest hearts of any wizard who ever lived, and I do not believe your heart told you to do this.

They hear a knock on the door.

Saved by the door.

She exits.

After a moment, DRACO enters, consumed by anger but hiding it well.

DRACO: I can't stay long. I won't need long.

HARRY: How can I help?

DRACO: I'm not here to antagonize you. But my son is in tears and I am his father and so I am here to ask why you would keep apart two good friends.

HARRY: I'm not keeping them apart.

DRACO: You've changed school timetables, you've threatened both teachers and Albus himself. Why?

HARRY looks at DRACO carefully and then turns away.

HARRY: I have to protect my son.

DRACO: From Scorpius?

HARRY: Bane told me he sensed a darkness around my son. Near my son.

DRACO: What are you implying, Potter?

HARRY turns and looks DRACO dead in the eye.

HARRY: Are you sure . . . are you really sure he's yours, Draco?

There's a deadly silence.

DRACO: You take that back . . . right now.

But HARRY doesn't take it back.

So DRACO takes his wand out.

HARRY: You do not want to do this.

DRACO: Yes, I do.

HARRY: I don't want to hurt you, Draco.

✦

DRACO: How interesting, because I do want to hurt you.

The two square up. And then release their wands.

DRACO and HARRY: Expelliarmus!

Their wands repel and then break apart.

DRACO: Incarcerous!

HARRY dodges a blast from DRACO's wand.

HARRY: Tarantallegra!

DRACO throws himself out of the way.

You've been practicing, Draco.

DRACO: And you've got sloppy, Potter. Densaugeo!

HARRY just manages to get out of the way.

HARRY: Rictusempra!

DRACO uses a chair to block the blast.

DRACO: Flipendo!

HARRY is sent twirling through the air. DRACO laughs.

Keep up, old man.

HARRY: We're the same age, Draco.

DRACO: I wear it better.

HARRY: Brachiabindo!

DRACO is bound tightly.

DRACO: That really the best you got? Emancipare.

DRACO releases his own binds.

Levicorpus!

HARRY has to throw himself out of the way.

Mobilicorpus! Oh, this is too much fun . . .

DRACO bounces HARRY up and down on the table. And then as HARRY rolls away, DRACO jumps onto the table—he readies his wand, but as he does, HARRY hits him with a spell . . .

HARRY: Obscuro!

DRACO releases himself from his blindfold as soon as it hits.

The two square up—HARRY throws a chair.

DRACO ducks underneath it and slows the chair with his wand.

GINNY: I only left this room three minutes ago!

She looks at the mess of the kitchen. She looks at the chairs suspended in the air. She signals them back to the floor with her wand.

(Drier than dry.) What did I miss?

ACT TWO, SCENE FOURTEEN

HOGWARTS, STAIRCASES

SCORPIUS walks unhappily down a staircase.

DELPHI scurries in from the other side.

DELPHI: So — technically — I shouldn't be here.

SCORPIUS: Delphi?

DELPHI: In fact, technically I'm endangering our entire operation . . . which is not . . . well, I'm not a natural risk-taker as you know. I've never been to Hogwarts. Pretty lax security here, isn't there? And so many portraits. And corridors. And ghosts! This half-headless, strange-looking ghost told me where I could find you, can you believe that?

SCORPIUS: You've never been to Hogwarts?

DELPHI: I was — unwell — as a child — for a few years. Other people got to go — I did not.

SCORPIUS: You were too — ill? I'm sorry, I didn't know that.

DELPHI: I don't advertise the fact — I prefer not to be seen as a tragic case, you know?

✦

This registers with SCORPIUS. He looks up to say something but DELPHI suddenly ducks from view as a student walks past. SCORPIUS tries to look casual until the student passes.

Have they gone?

SCORPIUS: Delphi, maybe it is too dangerous for you to be here —

DELPHI: Well — someone's got to do something about this.

SCORPIUS: Delphi, none of it worked, time-turning, we failed.

DELPHI: I know. Albus owled me. The history books changed but not enough — Cedric still died. In fact, failing the first task only made him more determined to win the second.

SCORPIUS: And Ron and Hermione have gone completely skewwhiff — and I still haven't figured out why.

DELPHI: And that's why Cedric has to wait. It's all become quite confused and you're entirely right to be keeping hold of the Time-Turner, Scorpius. But what I meant was — someone's got to do something about the two of you.

SCORPIUS: Oh.

DELPHI: You're best friends. Every owl he sends I can feel your absence. He's destroyed by it.

SCORPIUS: Sounds like he's found a shoulder to cry on. How many owls has he sent you now?

DELPHI smiles softly.

Sorry. That's—I didn't mean—I just—don't understand what's going on. I've tried to see him, talk to him, but every time I do he runs off.

DELPHI: You know, I didn't have a best friend when I was your age. I wanted one. Desperately. When I was younger I even invented one but—

SCORPIUS: I had one of those too. Called Flurry. We fell out over the correct rules of Gobstones.

DELPHI: Albus needs you, Scorpius. That's a wonderful thing.

SCORPIUS: He needs me to do what?

DELPHI: That's the thing, isn't it? About friendships. You don't know what he needs. You only know he needs it. Find him, Scorpius. You two—you belong together.

ACT TWO, SCENE FIFTEEN

HARRY AND GINNY POTTER'S HOUSE,
KITCHEN

HARRY and DRACO sit far apart. GINNY stands between them.

DRACO: Sorry about your kitchen, Ginny.

GINNY: Oh, it's not my kitchen. Harry does most of the cooking.

DRACO: I can't talk to him either. Scorpius. Especially since—Astoria
has gone. I can't even talk about how losing her has affected him.
As hard as I try, I can't reach him. You can't talk to Albus. I
can't talk to Scorpius. That's what this is about. Not about my
son being evil. Because as much as you might take the word of a
haughty centaur, you know the power of friendship.

HARRY: Draco, whatever you may think . . .

DRACO: I always envied you them, you know—Weasley and Granger.
I had—

GINNY: Crabbe and Goyle.

DRACO: Two lunks who wouldn't know one end of a broomstick from
another. You—the three of you—you shone, you know? You

liked each other. You had fun. I envied you those friendships more than anything else.

GINNY: I envied them too.

HARRY looks at GINNY, surprised.

HARRY: I need to protect him —

DRACO: My father thought he was protecting me. Most of the time. I think you have to make a choice — at a certain point — of the man you want to be. And I tell you that at that time you need a parent or a friend. And if you've learnt to hate your parent by then and you have no friends . . . then you're all alone. And being alone — that's so hard. I was alone. And it sent me to a truly dark place. For a long time. Tom Riddle was also a lonely child. You may not understand that, Harry, but I do — and I think Ginny does too.

GINNY: He's right.

DRACO: Tom Riddle didn't emerge from his dark place. And so Tom Riddle became Lord Voldemort. Maybe the black cloud Bane saw was Albus's loneliness. His pain. His hatred. Don't lose the boy. You'll regret it. And so will he. Because he needs you, and Scorpius, whether or not he now knows it.

HARRY looks at DRACO, he thinks.

He opens his mouth to speak. He thinks.

GINNY: Harry. Will you get the Floo powder or shall I?

HARRY looks up at his wife.

ACT TWO, SCENE SIXTEEN

HOGWARTS, LIBRARY

SCORPIUS arrives in the library. He looks left and right. And then he sees ALBUS. And ALBUS sees him.

SCORPIUS: Hi.

ALBUS: Scorpius. I can't . . .

SCORPIUS: I know. You're in Gryffindor now. You don't want to see me now. But here I am anyway. Talking to you.

ALBUS: Well, I can't talk so . . .

SCORPIUS: You have to. You think you can just ignore everything that's happened? The world has gone crazy, have you noticed?

ALBUS: I know, okay? Ron's gone strange. Hermione's a professor, it's all wrong, but . . .

SCORPIUS: And Rose doesn't exist.

ALBUS: I know. Look, I don't understand everything but you can't be here.

SCORPIUS: Because of what we did, Rose wasn't even born. Do you remember being told about the Triwizard Tournament Yule Ball? All the four Triwizard champions took a partner. Your dad took Parvati Patil, Viktor Krum took—

ALBUS: Hermione. And Ron got jealous and behaved like a prat.

SCORPIUS: Only he didn't. I found Rita Skeeter's book about them. And it's very different. Ron took Hermione to the ball.

ALBUS: What?

POLLY CHAPMAN: Sshhhh!

SCORPIUS looks at POLLY and drops his volume.

SCORPIUS: As friends. And they danced in a friendly way, and it was nice, and then he danced with Padma Patil and that was nicer, and they started dating and he changed a bit and then they got married and meanwhile Hermione became a—

ALBUS: —psychopath.

SCORPIUS: Hermione was supposed to go to that ball with Krum—do you know why she didn't? Because she had suspicions the two strange Durmstrang boys she met before the first task were somehow involved in the disappearance of Cedric's wand. She believed we—under Viktor's orders—cost Cedric the first task . . .

ALBUS: Wow.

SCORPIUS: And without Krum, Ron never got jealous and that jealousy was all-important and so Ron and Hermione stayed very good friends but never fell in love—never got married—*never had Rose.*

ALBUS: So that's why Dad's so—did he change too?

SCORPIUS: I'm pretty sure your dad is exactly the same. Head of
Magical Law Enforcement. Married to Ginny. Three kids.

ALBUS: So why is he being such a—

A LIBRARIAN enters at the back of the room.

SCORPIUS: Have you heard me, Albus? This is bigger than you and
your dad. Professor Croaker's law—the furthest someone can go
back in time without the possibility of serious harm to the traveler
or time itself is five hours. And we went back years. The smallest
moment, the smallest change, it creates ripples. And we—we've
created really bad ripples. Rose was never born because of what
we did. Rose.

LIBRARIAN: Ssshhh!

ALBUS thinks quickly.

ALBUS: Fine, let's go back—fix it. Get Cedric and Rose back.

SCORPIUS: . . . is the wrong answer.

ALBUS: You've still got the Time-Turner, right? No one found it?

SCORPIUS takes it out of his pocket.

SCORPIUS: Yes, but . . .

ALBUS snatches it from his hand.

No. Don't . . . Albus. Don't you understand how bad things
could get?

⚜

SCORPIUS grabs for the Time-Turner, ALBUS pushes him back, they wrestle inexpertly.

ALBUS: Things need fixing, Scorpius. Cedric still needs saving. Rose needs bringing back. We'll be more careful. Whatever Croaker says, trust me, trust us. We'll get it right this time.

SCORPIUS: No. We won't. Give it back, Albus! Give it back!

ALBUS: I can't. This is too important.

SCORPIUS: Yes, it's too important—for us. We're not good at this stuff. We'll get it wrong.

ALBUS: Who's saying that we'll get it wrong?

SCORPIUS: *I* say. Because that's *what we do.* We mess things up. We lose. We're losers, true and total losers. Haven't you realized that yet?

ALBUS finally gets the upper hand and pins SCORPIUS to the ground.

ALBUS: Well, I wasn't a loser before I met you.

SCORPIUS: Albus, whatever you've got to prove to your dad—this isn't the way.

ALBUS: I don't have anything to prove to my dad. I've got to save Cedric to save Rose. And maybe—without you holding me back—I can make a proper go of it.

SCORPIUS: Without me? Oh poor Albus Potter. With his chip on his shoulder. Poor Albus Potter. So sad.

ALBUS: What are you saying?

140

SCORPIUS *(exploding)*: Try my life! People look at you because your dad's the famous Harry Potter, savior of the wizarding world. People look at me because they think my dad is Voldemort. Voldemort.

ALBUS: Don't even —

SCORPIUS: Can you even slightly imagine what that's like? Have you even ever tried? No. Because you can't see beyond the end of your nose. Because you can't see beyond the end of your stupid thing with your dad. He will always be Harry Potter, you know that, right? And you will always be his son. And I know it's hard, and the other kids are awful, but you have to learn to be okay with that, because — there are worse things, okay?

Beat.

There was a moment I was excited, when I realized time was different, a moment when I thought maybe my mum hadn't got sick. Maybe my mum wasn't dead. But no, turns out, she was. I'm still the child of Voldemort, without a mother, giving sympathy to the boy who doesn't ever give anything back. So I'm sorry if I've ruined your life because I tell you — you wouldn't have a chance of ruining mine — it was already ruined. You just didn't make it better. Because you're a terrible — the most terrible — friend.

ALBUS digests this. He sees what he's done to his friend.

PROFESSOR McGONAGALL *(from off)*: Albus? Albus Potter. Scorpius Malfoy. Are you in there — together? Because I advise you not to be.

ALBUS looks at SCORPIUS, he pulls a Cloak from his bag.

ALBUS: Quick. We need to hide.

SCORPIUS: What?

ALBUS: Scorpius, look at me.

SCORPIUS: That's the Invisibility Cloak? Isn't it James's?

ALBUS: If she finds us, we'll be forced apart forever. Please. I didn't understand. Please.

PROFESSOR McGONAGALL (*from off — trying to give them every chance*): I am about to enter.

PROFESSOR McGONAGALL comes into the room, the Marauder's Map in her hands. The boys disappear beneath the Cloak. She looks around, exasperated.

Well, where have they — I never wanted this thing and now it's playing tricks on me.

She thinks. She looks back at the map. She identifies where they should be. She looks around the room. Objects move as the boys invisibly move past them. She sees where they're heading, she makes to block them. But they skirt around her.

Unless. Unless . . . Your father's Cloak.

She looks back at the map, she looks at the boys. She smiles to herself.

Well, if I didn't see you, I didn't see you.

She exits. The two boys remove the Cloak. They sit in silence for a moment.

ALBUS: Yes, I stole this from James. He's remarkably easy to steal from; his trunk combination is the date he got his first broom. I've found the Cloak made avoiding bullies . . . easier.

SCORPIUS nods.

I'm sorry—about your mum. I know we don't talk about her enough—but I hope you know—I'm sorry—it's rubbish—what happened to her—to you.

SCORPIUS: Thanks.

ALBUS: My dad said—said that you were this dark cloud around me. My dad started to think—and I just knew I had to stay away, and if I didn't, Dad said he would—

SCORPIUS: Your dad thinks the rumors are true—I am the son of Voldemort?

ALBUS *(nods)*: His department are currently investigating it.

SCORPIUS: Good. Let them. Sometimes—sometimes I find myself thinking—maybe they're true too.

ALBUS: No. They're not true. And I'll tell you why. Because I don't think Voldemort is capable of having a kind son—and you're kind, Scorpius. To the depths of your belly, to the tips of your fingers. I truly believe Voldemort—Voldemort couldn't have a child like you.

Beat. SCORPIUS is moved by this.

SCORPIUS: That's nice—that's a nice thing to say.

ALBUS: And it's something I should have said a long time ago. In fact, you're probably the best person I know. And you don't—you couldn't—hold me back. You make me stronger—and when Dad forced us apart—without you—

SCORPIUS: I didn't much like my life without you in it either.

ALBUS: And I know I'll always be Harry Potter's son—and I will sort that out in my head—and I know compared to you my life is pretty good, really, and that he and I are comparatively lucky and—

SCORPIUS *(interrupting)*: Albus, as apologies go this is wonderfully fulsome, but you're starting to talk more about *you* than *me* again, so probably better to quit while you're ahead.

ALBUS smiles and stretches out a hand.

ALBUS: Friends?

SCORPIUS: Always.

SCORPIUS extends his hand, ALBUS pulls SCORPIUS up into a hug.

That's the second time you've done that.

The two boys break apart and smile.

ALBUS: But I'm pleased we had this argument because it's given me a really good idea.

SCORPIUS: About what?

ALBUS: It involves the second task. And humiliation.

SCORPIUS: You're still talking about going back in time? Have we been having the same conversation?

ALBUS: You're right—we are losers. We're brilliant at losing and so we should be using our own knowledge here. Our own powers. Losers are taught to be losers. And there's only one way to teach a loser—and we know that better than anyone—humiliation. We need to humiliate him. So in the second task that's what we'll do.

SCORPIUS thinks—for a long time—and then smiles.

SCORPIUS: That's a really good strategy.

ALBUS: I know.

SCORPIUS: I mean, quite spectacular. Humiliate Cedric to save Cedric. Clever. And Rose?

ALBUS: That I'm saving as a sparkly surprise. I *can* do it without you— but I *want* you there. Because I want us to do this together. Set things right together. So . . . Will you come?

SCORPIUS: But, just a minute, isn't—wasn't—the second task took place in the lake, and you're not allowed to leave the school building.

ALBUS grins.

ALBUS: Yes. About that . . . We need to find the girls' bathroom on the first floor.

ACT TWO, SCENE SEVENTEEN

HOGWARTS, STAIRCASES

RON is walking down the staircase, consumed in his thoughts, and then he sees HERMIONE and his expression changes entirely.

RON: Professor Granger.

HERMIONE looks across, her heart leaps a bit too (though she won't admit it).

HERMIONE: Ron. What are you doing here?

RON: Panju got in a little trouble in Potions class. Was showing off, of course, and put the wrong thing with the wrong thing and now he has no eyebrows and a rather large mustache, apparently. Which doesn't suit him. I didn't want to come but Padma says that when it comes to facial growths, sons need their fathers. Have you done something with your hair?

HERMIONE: Just combed it, I suspect.

RON: Well . . . Combing it suits you.

HERMIONE looks at RON slightly strangely.

HERMIONE: Ron, will you stop looking at me like that?

RON *(summoning confidence)*: You know, Harry's boy Albus—said to me the other day that he thought you and I were—married. Ha-ha. Ha. Ha. Ridiculous, I know.

HERMIONE: Very ridiculous.

RON: He even thought we had a daughter. That'd be strange, wouldn't it?

The two lock eyes. HERMIONE is the first to break away.

HERMIONE: More than strange.

RON: Exactly. We're—friends, and that's all.

HERMIONE: Absolutely. Only—friends.

RON: Only—friends. Funny word—*friends*. Not that funny. Just a word really. Friends. Friend. Funny friend. You, my funny friend, my Hermione. Not that—not my Hermione, you understand—not MY Hermione—not MINE—you know, but . . .

HERMIONE: I know.

There's a pause. Neither of them move the smallest inch. Everything feels too important for movement. Then RON coughs.

RON: Well. Must get on. Sort Panju out. Teach him the finer arts of mustache grooming.

He walks on, he turns, he looks at HERMIONE. She looks back, he hurries on again.

Your hair really does very much suit you.

ACT TWO, SCENE EIGHTEEN

HOGWARTS, HEADMISTRESS'S OFFICE

PROFESSOR McGONAGALL is onstage on her own. She looks at the map. She frowns to herself. She taps it with her wand. She smiles to herself at a good decision made.

PROFESSOR McGONAGALL: Mischief managed.

> *There's a rattling.*

> *The whole stage seems to vibrate.*

> *GINNY is the first through the fireplace, and then HARRY.*

GINNY: Professor, I can't say that ever gets more dignified.

PROFESSOR McGONAGALL: Potter. You're back. And you seem to have finally ruined my carpet.

HARRY: I need to find my son. We need to.

PROFESSOR McGONAGALL: Harry, I've considered this and decided I want no part of it. Whatever you threaten, I —

HARRY: Minerva, I come here in peace, not war. I should never have spoken to you that way.

PROFESSOR McGONAGALL: I just don't think I can interfere in friendships and I believe —

HARRY: I need to say sorry to you and sorry to Albus, will you give me that chance?

DRACO arrives behind them with a bang of soot.

PROFESSOR McGONAGALL: Draco?

DRACO: He needs to see his son, and I need to see mine.

HARRY: Like I say — peace — not war.

PROFESSOR McGONAGALL studies his face; she sees the sincerity she needs to see. She takes the map back out of her pocket. She opens it up.

PROFESSOR McGONAGALL: Well, peace is certainly something I can be part of.

She taps it with her wand.

(Sighs.) I solemnly swear that I'm up to no good.

The map is lit into action.

Well, they are together.

DRACO: In the girls' bathroom on the first floor. What on earth would they be doing there?

ACT TWO, SCENE NINETEEN

HOGWARTS, GIRLS' BATHROOM

SCORPIUS and ALBUS enter a bathroom. In the center of it is a large Victorian sink.

SCORPIUS: So let me get this right—the plan is Engorgement . . .

ALBUS: Yes. Scorpius, that soap, if you may . . .

SCORPIUS fishes a soap out of the sink.

Engorgio.

He fires a bolt from his wand across the room. The soap blows up to four times its size.

SCORPIUS: Nice. Consider me engorgimpressed.

ALBUS: The second task was the lake task. They had to retrieve something which was stolen from them, which turned out to be—

SCORPIUS: —people they loved.

ALBUS: Cedric used a Bubble-Head Charm to swim through the lake. All we do is follow him in there and use Engorgement to turn him into something rather larger. We know the Time-Turner doesn't give us long, so we're going to be quick. Get to him and Engorgio his head and watch him float out of the lake — away from the task — away from the competition . . .

SCORPIUS: But — you still haven't told me how we're going to actually get to the lake . . .

And then suddenly a jet of water emerges from the sink — and after it ascends a very wet MOANING MYRTLE.

MOANING MYRTLE: Whoa. That feels good. Never used to enjoy that. But when you get to my age, you take what you can . . .

SCORPIUS: Of course — you're a genius — Moaning Myrtle . . .

MOANING MYRTLE swoops down onto SCORPIUS.

MOANING MYRTLE: What did you call me? Do I moan? Am I moaning now? AM I? AM I?

SCORPIUS: No, I didn't mean . . .

MOANING MYRTLE: What's my name?

SCORPIUS: Myrtle.

MOANING MYRTLE: Exactly — Myrtle. Myrtle Elizabeth Warren — a pretty name — my name — no need for the moaning.

SCORPIUS: Well . . .

MOANING MYRTLE *(she giggles)*: It's been a while. Boys. In my bathroom. In my girls' bathroom. Well, that's not right . . . But then again, I always did have a soft spot for the Potters. And I was moderately partial to a Malfoy too. Now how can I help you pair?

ALBUS: You were there, Myrtle — in the lake. They wrote about you. There must be a way out of these pipes.

MOANING MYRTLE: I've been everywhere. But where specifically were you thinking?

ALBUS: The second task. The lake task. In the Triwizard Tournament. Twenty-five years ago. Harry and Cedric.

MOANING MYRTLE: Such a shame the pretty one had to die. Not that your father is not pretty — but Cedric Diggory — you'd be amazed at how many girls I had to hear doing love incantations in this very bathroom . . . And the weeping after he was taken.

ALBUS: Help us, Myrtle, help us get into that same lake.

MOANING MYRTLE: You think I can help you travel in time?

ALBUS: We need you to keep a secret.

MOANING MYRTLE: I love secrets. I won't tell a soul. Cross my heart and hope to die. Or — the equivalent. For ghosts. You know.

ALBUS nods at SCORPIUS, who reveals the Time-Turner.

ALBUS: We can travel in time. You're going to help us travel the pipes. We're going to save Cedric Diggory.

MOANING MYRTLE *(grins)*: Well, that sounds like fun.

ALBUS: And we've no time to lose.

MOANING MYRTLE: This very sink. This very sink empties directly into the lake. It breaks every bylaw but this school has always been antiquated. Dive in and you will be piped straight to it.

ALBUS pulls himself into the sink, dumping his cloak as he does. SCORPIUS copies.

ALBUS hands SCORPIUS some green foliage in a bag.

ALBUS: Some for me and some for you.

SCORPIUS: Gillyweed? We're using gillyweed? To breathe underwater?

ALBUS: Just like my dad did. Now, are you ready?

SCORPIUS: Remember, this time we can't be caught out by the clock . . .

ALBUS: Five minutes, that's all we allow for—before we get pulled back to the present.

SCORPIUS: Tell me this is all going to be okay.

ALBUS *(grinning)*: It's all going to be entirely okay. Are you ready?

ALBUS takes the gillyweed and disappears down.

SCORPIUS: No, Albus—Albus—

He looks up, he and MOANING MYRTLE are alone.

MOANING MYRTLE: I do like brave boys.

SCORPIUS *(a little bit scared, a tiny bit brave)*: Then I'm entirely ready. For whatever comes.

He takes the gillyweed and disappears down.

MOANING MYRTLE is left alone onstage.

There is a giant whoosh of light and smash of noise. And time stops. And then it turns over, thinks a bit, and begins spooling backwards . . .

The boys are gone.

HARRY appears at a run, a deep frown on his face, behind him DRACO, GINNY, and PROFESSOR McGONAGALL.

HARRY: Albus . . . Albus . . .

GINNY: He's gone.

They find the boys' cloaks on the ground.

PROFESSOR McGONAGALL *(consulting the map)*: He's disappeared. No, he's traveling under Hogwarts grounds, no, he's disappeared . . .

DRACO: How is he doing this?

MOANING MYRTLE: He's using a rather pretty trinket thingy.

HARRY: Myrtle!

MOANING MYRTLE: Oops, you caught me. And I was trying so hard to hide. Hello, Harry. Hello, Draco. Have you been bad boys again?

HARRY: What trinket is he using?

MOANING MYRTLE: I think it was a secret, but I could never keep anything from you, Harry. How is it you've grown handsomer and handsomer as you've aged? And you're taller.

HARRY: My son is in danger. I need your help. What are they doing, Myrtle?

MOANING MYRTLE: He's after saving a dishy boy. A certain Cedric Diggory.

HARRY immediately realizes what's happened, and is horrified.

PROFESSOR McGONAGALL: But Cedric Diggory died years ago . . .

MOANING MYRTLE: He seemed quite confident he could get around that fact. He's very confident, Harry, just like you.

HARRY: He heard me talking—to Amos Diggory . . . could he have . . . the Ministry's Time-Turner. No, that's impossible.

PROFESSOR McGONAGALL: The Ministry has a Time-Turner? I thought they were destroyed?

MOANING MYRTLE: Isn't everyone so naughty?

DRACO: Can someone please explain what's going on?

HARRY: Albus and Scorpius are not disappearing and reappearing— they're traveling. Traveling in time.

ACT TWO, SCENE TWENTY

TRIWIZARD TOURNAMENT, LAKE, 1995

LUDO BAGMAN: Ladies and gentlemen—boys and girls—I give you—the greatest—the fabulous—the one—and the only **TRIWIZARD TOURNAMENT**. If you're from Hogwarts. Give me a cheer.

There's a loud cheer.

And now ALBUS and SCORPIUS are swimming through the lake. Descending through the water with graceful ease.

If you're from Durmstrang—give me a cheer.

There's a loud cheer.

AND IF YOU'RE FROM BEAUXBATONS GIVE ME A CHEER.

There's a slightly less limp cheer.

The French are getting into this.

And they're off . . . Viktor's a shark, of course he is, Fleur looks remarkable, ever plucky Harry is using gillyweed, clever Harry, very clever—and Cedric—well, Cedric, what a treat, ladies and gentlemen, Cedric is using a Bubble Charm to cruise through the lake.

CEDRIC DIGGORY approaches them through the water, a bubble over his head. ALBUS and SCORPIUS raise their wands together and fire an Engorgement Charm through the water.

He turns and looks at them, confused. And it hits him. And around him the water glows gold.

And then CEDRIC starts to grow — and grow again — and grow some more. He looks around himself — entirely panicked. And the boys watch as CEDRIC ascends helplessly through the water.

But no, what's this . . . Cedric Diggory is ascending out of the water and seemingly out of the competition. Oh, ladies and gentlemen, we don't have our winner but we certainly have our loser. Cedric Diggory is turning into a balloon, and this balloon wants to fly. Fly, ladies and gentlemen, fly. Fly out of the task and out of the tournament and — oh my, it gets wilder still, around Cedric, fireworks *explode* declaiming — "Ron loves Hermione" — and the crowd love that — oh, ladies and gentlemen, the look on Cedric's face. It's quite some picture, it's quite some sight, it's quite some tragedy. This is a humiliation, there's no other word for it.

And ALBUS smiles widely and high-fives SCORPIUS in the water.

And ALBUS points up, and SCORPIUS nods, and they start to swim ever upwards. And as CEDRIC ascends, people start to laugh, and everything changes.

The world becomes darker. The world becomes almost black, in fact.

✦

And there's a flash. And a bang. And the Time-Turner ticks to a stop. And we're back in the present.

SCORPIUS suddenly emerges, shooting up through the water. And he's triumphant.

SCORPIUS: Woooo-hoooooo!

He looks around, surprised. Where's ALBUS? He puts his arms into the air.

We did it!

He waits another beat.

Albus?

ALBUS still doesn't emerge. SCORPIUS treads water, he thinks and then he ducks back into the water.

He emerges back up again. Now thoroughly panicked. He looks around.

Albus . . . ALBUS . . . ALBUS.

And there's a whisper in Parseltongue. Which travels fast around the audience.

He's coming. He's coming. He's coming.

DOLORES UMBRIDGE: Scorpius Malfoy. Get out of the lake. Get out of the lake. Right now.

She pulls him out of the water.

SCORPIUS: Miss. I need help. Please, Miss.

DOLORES UMBRIDGE: Miss? I'm Professor Umbridge, the headmistress of your school, I'm no "Miss."

SCORPIUS: You're the headmistress? But I . . .

꙳

DOLORES UMBRIDGE: I am the headmistress, and however important your family may be—it doesn't give you an excuse to dillydally, to mess about.

SCORPIUS: There's a boy in this lake. You need to get help. I'm looking for my friend, Miss. Professor. Headmaster. One of Hogwarts's students, Miss. I'm looking for Albus Potter.

DOLORES UMBRIDGE: Potter? Albus Potter? There's no such student. In fact, there hasn't been a Potter at Hogwarts for years—and that boy didn't turn out so well. Not so much rest in peace, Harry Potter, more rest in perpetual despair. Total troublemaker.

SCORPIUS: Harry Potter's dead?

Suddenly from around the auditorium, the feel of a breath of the wind. Some black robes arise around people. Black robes that become black shapes. That become dementors.

Flying dementors through the auditorium. These black deadly shapes, these black deadly forces. They are everything to be feared. And they suck the spirit from the room.

The wind continues. This is hell. And then, right from the back of the room, whispering around everyone.

Words said with an unmistakable voice. The voice of VOLDEMORT . . .

Haaarry Potttter.

HARRY's dream has come to life.

DOLORES UMBRIDGE: Have you swallowed something funny in there? Become a Mudblood without any of us noticing? Harry Potter died over twenty years ago as part of that failed coup on the school—he was one of those Dumbledore terrorists we bravely overthrew at the Battle of Hogwarts. Now come along—I don't know what game you're playing but you're upsetting the dementors and entirely ruining Voldemort Day.

And the Parseltongue whispers grow louder and louder. Grow monstrously loud. And giant banners with snake symbols upon them descend over the stage.

SCORPIUS: Voldemort Day?

We cut to black.

HARRY POTTER
AND THE
CURSED CHILD

※

PART TWO

ACT THREE

ACT THREE, SCENE ONE

HOGWARTS, HEADMISTRESS'S OFFICE

SCORPIUS enters the office of DOLORES UMBRIDGE. He is dressed in darker, blacker robes. He has a pensive look on his face. He remains coiled and alert.

DOLORES UMBRIDGE: Scorpius. Thank you so much for coming to see me.

SCORPIUS: Headmistress.

DOLORES UMBRIDGE: Scorpius, I've thought for a long time that you have Head Boy potential, as you know. Pure-blooded, a natural leader, wonderfully athletic . . .

SCORPIUS: Athletic?

DOLORES UMBRIDGE: No need to be modest, Scorpius. I've seen you on the Quidditch pitch, there's rarely a Snitch you don't catch. You are a highly valued student. Valued by the faculty. Valued especially by me. I've positively glowed about you in dispatches to the Augurey. Our work together flushing out the more dilettante students has made this school a safer, purer place—

SCORPIUS: Has it?

There is the sound of a scream from off. SCORPIUS turns towards it. But he dismisses the thought. He must and he will control himself.

DOLORES UMBRIDGE: But in the three days since I found you in that lake on Voldemort Day, you've become . . . odder and odder. In particular, this sudden obsession with Harry Potter . . .

SCORPIUS: I don't . . .

DOLORES UMBRIDGE: Questioning everyone you can about the Battle of Hogwarts. How Potter died. Why Potter died. And this ludicrous fascination with Cedric Diggory. Scorpius, we've checked you for hexes and curses — there were none we can see — so I'm asking if there's anything I can do — to restore you to what you were . . .

SCORPIUS: No. No. Consider me restored. Temporary aberration. That's all.

DOLORES UMBRIDGE: So we can continue our work together?

SCORPIUS: We can.

She puts her hand to her heart, and touches her wrists together.

DOLORES UMBRIDGE: For Voldemort and Valor.

SCORPIUS *(trying to copy)*: For — um — yes.

ACT THREE, SCENE TWO

HOGWARTS, GROUNDS

KARL JENKINS: Hey, Scorpion King.

SCORPIUS is high-fived, it's painful, he takes it.

YANN FREDERICKS: We're still on, right, tomorrow night?

KARL JENKINS: Because we are ready to spill some proper Mudblood guts.

POLLY CHAPMAN: Scorpius.

POLLY CHAPMAN is standing on the stairs, SCORPIUS turns towards her, surprised to hear her say his name.

SCORPIUS: Polly Chapman?

POLLY CHAPMAN: Shall we cut to it? I know everyone is waiting to know who you're going to ask because, you know, you need to ask someone and I've been asked by three people already and I know I'm not alone in refusing them all. In case, you know, you were to ask me.

SCORPIUS: Right.

POLLY CHAPMAN: Which would be great. If you were interested. Which rumor is—you are. And I just want to make clear—at this moment—that I am also interested. And that isn't a rumor. That's a—f-a-c-t—fact.

SCORPIUS: That's um—great but—what are we talking about?

POLLY CHAPMAN: The Blood Ball, of course. Who you—the Scorpion King—are taking to the Blood Ball.

SCORPIUS: You—Polly Chapman—want me to take you to a—ball?

There is the sound of screaming behind him.

What is that screaming?

POLLY CHAPMAN: Mudbloods, of course. In the dungeons. Your idea, wasn't it? What's going on with you? Oh Potter, I've got blood on my shoes again . . .

She bends and carefully cleans the blood off her shoes.

Like the Augurey insists—the future is ours to make—so here I am, making a future—with you. For Voldemort and Valor.

SCORPIUS: For Voldemort it is.

POLLY walks on, SCORPIUS looks agonized after her. What is this world—and what is he within it?

ACT THREE, SCENE THREE

MINISTRY OF MAGIC,
OFFICE OF THE HEAD OF
MAGICAL LAW ENFORCEMENT

DRACO is impressive in a way we haven't seen. He has the smell of power about him. Flying down either side of the room are Augurey flags — with the bird emblazoned in a fascistic manner.

DRACO: You are late.

SCORPIUS: This is your office?

DRACO: You are late and unapologetic, maybe you are determined to compound the problem.

SCORPIUS: You're Head of Magical Law Enforcement?

DRACO: How dare you! How dare you embarrass me and keep me waiting and then not apologize for it!

SCORPIUS: Sorry.

DRACO: *Sir.*

SCORPIUS: Sorry, sir.

DRACO: I did not bring you up to be sloppy, Scorpius. I did not bring you up to humiliate me at Hogwarts.

SCORPIUS: Humiliate you, sir?

DRACO: Harry Potter, asking questions about Harry Potter, of all the embarrassing things. How dare you disgrace the Malfoy name.

SCORPIUS: Oh no. Are you responsible? No. No. You can't be.

DRACO: Scorpius . . .

SCORPIUS: The *Daily Prophet* today — three wizards blowing up bridges to see how many Muggles they can kill with one blast — is that you?

DRACO: Be very careful.

SCORPIUS: The "Mudblood" death camps, the torture, the burning alive of those that oppose him. How much of that is you? Mum always told me that you were a better man than I could see, but this is what you really are, isn't it? A murderer, a torturer, a —

DRACO rises up and pulls SCORPIUS hard onto the table. The violence is surprising and deadly.

DRACO: Do not use her name in vain, Scorpius. Do not score points that way. She deserves better than that.

SCORPIUS says nothing, horrified and scared. DRACO reads this. He lets go of SCORPIUS's head. He doesn't like hurting his son.

And no, those idiots blasting Muggles, that's not my doing, though it'll be me the Augurey asks to bribe the Muggle Prime Minister with gold . . . Did your mother really say that of me?

SCORPIUS: She said that Grandfather didn't like her very much—opposed the match—thought she was too Muggle-loving—too weak—but that you defied him for her. She said it was the bravest thing she'd ever seen.

DRACO: She made being brave very easy, your mother.

SCORPIUS: But that was—another you.

He looks at his dad, who looks back with a frown.

I've done bad things, you've done worse. What have we become, Dad?

DRACO: We haven't become anything—we simply are as we are.

SCORPIUS: The Malfoys. The family you can always rely on to make the world a murkier place.

This hits home with DRACO. He looks carefully at SCORPIUS.

DRACO: This business at the school—what's inspired it?

SCORPIUS: I don't want to be who I am.

DRACO: And what's brought that on?

SCORPIUS desperately thinks for a way of describing his story.

SCORPIUS: I've seen myself in a different way.

DRACO: You know what I loved most about your mother? She could always help me find light in the darkness. She made the world—my world, anyway—less—what was the word you used—"murky."

SCORPIUS: Did she?

DRACO studies his son.

DRACO: There's more of her in there than I thought.

Beat. He looks at SCORPIUS carefully.

Whatever you're doing — do it safely. I can't lose you too.

SCORPIUS: Yes. Sir.

DRACO looks at his son one last time — trying to understand his head.

DRACO: For Voldemort and Valor.

SCORPIUS looks at him and backs out of the room.

SCORPIUS: For Voldemort and Valor.

ACT THREE, SCENE FOUR

HOGWARTS, LIBRARY

SCORPIUS enters the library and starts desperately to look through books. He finds a history book.

SCORPIUS: How did Cedric become a Death Eater? What have I missed? Find me some—light in the darkness. Tell me your secrets. What have I missed?

CRAIG BOWKER JR.: Why are you here?

SCORPIUS turns to look at a rather desperate-looking CRAIG, his clothes tattered and worn.

SCORPIUS: Why can't I be here?

CRAIG BOWKER JR.: It's not ready yet. I'm working as fast as I can. But Professor Snape sets so much of it, and writing the essay in two different ways. I mean, I'm not complaining . . . Sorry.

SCORPIUS: Start again. From the beginning. What's not ready?

CRAIG BOWKER JR.: Your Potions homework. And I'm happy to do it—grateful even—and I know you hate homework and books and I never let you down, you know that.

SCORPIUS: I hate homework?

CRAIG BOWKER JR.: You're the Scorpion King. Of course you hate homework. What are you doing with *A History of Magic*? I could do that assignment too?

Pause. SCORPIUS looks at CRAIG a moment and then walks away. CRAIG exits.

After a moment SCORPIUS returns with a frown.

SCORPIUS: Did he say Snape?

ACT THREE, SCENE FIVE

HOGWARTS, POTIONS CLASSROOM

SCORPIUS runs into the Potions classroom, slamming back the door. SEVERUS SNAPE looks up at him.

SNAPE: Did no one teach you to knock, boy?

> *SCORPIUS looks up at SNAPE, slightly breathless, slightly unsure, slightly exultant.*

SCORPIUS: Severus Snape. This is an honor.

SNAPE: Professor Snape will do fine. You may behave like a king at this school, Malfoy, but that doesn't make us all your subjects.

SCORPIUS: But you're the answer . . .

SNAPE: How very pleasant for me. If you've got something to say, boy, then please say it . . . If not, close the door on your way out.

SCORPIUS: I need your help.

SNAPE: I exist to serve.

SCORPIUS: I just don't know what help I — need. Are you still undercover now? Are you still working secretly for Dumbledore?

SNAPE: Dumbledore? Dumbledore's dead. And my work for him was public — I taught in his school.

SCORPIUS: No. That's not all you did. You watched the Death Eaters for him. You advised him. Everyone thought you'd murdered him — but it turned out you'd been supporting him. You saved the world.

SNAPE: These are very dangerous allegations, boy. And don't think the Malfoy name will prevent me inflicting punishment.

SCORPIUS: What if I was to tell you there was another world — another world in which Voldemort was defeated at the Battle of Hogwarts, in which Harry Potter and Dumbledore's Army won, how would you feel then . . .

SNAPE: I'd say that the rumors of Hogwarts's beloved Scorpion King losing his mind are well-founded.

SCORPIUS: There was a stolen Time-Turner. I stole a Time-Turner. With Albus. We tried to bring Cedric Diggory back from the dead, when he was dead. We tried to stop him winning the Triwizard Tournament. But by doing so we turned him into an almost different person entirely.

SNAPE: Harry Potter won that Triwizard Tournament.

SCORPIUS: He wasn't supposed to do it alone. Cedric was supposed to win it with him. But we humiliated him out of the tournament. And as a result of that humiliation he became a Death Eater. I can't work out what he did in the Battle of Hogwarts — whether he killed someone or — but he did something and it changed everything.

SNAPE: Cedric Diggory killed only one wizard and not a significant one — Neville Longbottom.

SCORPIUS: Oh, of course, that's it! Professor Longbottom was supposed to kill Nagini, Voldemort's snake. Nagini had to die before Voldemort could die. That's it! You've solved it! We destroyed Cedric, he killed Neville, Voldemort won the battle. Can you see? Can you see it?

SNAPE: I can see this is a Malfoy game. Get out before I alert your father and plunge you into deep trouble.

SCORPIUS thinks and then plays his final, desperate card.

SCORPIUS: You loved his mother. I don't remember everything. I know you loved his mother. Harry's mother. Lily. I know you spent years undercover. I know without you the war could never have been won. How would I know this if I hadn't seen the other world . . . ?

SNAPE says nothing, overwhelmed.

Only Dumbledore knew, am I right? And when you lost him you must have felt so alone. I know you're a good man. Harry Potter told his son you're a great man.

SNAPE looks at SCORPIUS — unsure what's going on. Is this a trick? He is quite seriously at a loss.

SNAPE: Harry Potter is dead.

SCORPIUS: Not in my world. He said you were the bravest man he'd ever met. He knew, you see — he knew your secret — what you did for Dumbledore. And he admired you for it — greatly. And that's why he named his son — my best friend — after you both. Albus Severus Potter.

SNAPE is stopped. He is deeply moved.

Please — for Lily, for the world, help me.

SNAPE thinks and then walks up to SCORPIUS, taking out his wand as he does. SCORPIUS steps back, scared. SNAPE fires his wand at the door.

SNAPE: Colloportus!

An invisible lock slams into place. SNAPE opens a hatch at the back of the classroom.

Well, come on, then . . .

SCORPIUS: Just a question, but where — exactly — are we going?

SNAPE: We've had to move many times. Everywhere we've settled they destroyed. This will take us to a room hidden in the roots of the Whomping Willow.

SCORPIUS: Okay, who's we?

SNAPE: Oh. You'll see.

ACT THREE, SCENE SIX

CAMPAIGN ROOM

SCORPIUS is pinned to the table by a magnificent-looking HERMIONE. Her clothes faded, her eyes blazing, she is full warrior now and it rather suits her.

HERMIONE: You make one more move and your brain will be a frog and your arms will be rubber.

SNAPE: Safe. He's safe. *(Beat.)* You know you never could listen. You were a terrible bore of a student and you're a terrible bore of—whatever you are.

HERMIONE: I was an excellent student.

SNAPE: You were moderate to average. He's on our side!

SCORPIUS: I am, Hermione.

HERMIONE looks at SCORPIUS, still very distrustful.

HERMIONE: Most people know me as Granger. And I don't believe a word you say, Malfoy—

SCORPIUS: It's all my fault. My fault. And Albus's.

HERMIONE: Albus? Albus Dumbledore? What's Albus Dumbledore got to do with this?

SNAPE: He doesn't mean Dumbledore. You may need to sit down.

RON runs in. His hair spiked. His clothes scruffy. He is slightly less good at the rebel look than HERMIONE is.

RON: Snape, a royal visit, and — *(he sees SCORPIUS and is immediately alarmed)* what's he doing here?

He fumbles out his wand.

I'm armed and — entirely dangerous and seriously advise you —

He realizes his wand is the wrong way around and turns it right.

To be very careful —

SNAPE: He's safe, Ron.

RON looks at HERMIONE, who nods.

RON: Thank Dumbledore for that.

ACT THREE, SCENE SEVEN

CAMPAIGN ROOM

HERMIONE is sitting studying the Time-Turner as RON tries to digest it all.

RON: So you're telling me that the whole of history rests on . . . Neville Longbottom? This is pretty wild.

HERMIONE: It's true, Ron.

RON: Right. And you're sure because . . .

HERMIONE: What he knows about Snape — about all of us — there's no way he could . . .

RON: Maybe he's a really good guesser?

SCORPIUS: I'm not. Can you help?

RON: We're the only ones that can. Dumbledore's Army has shrunk considerably since its peak. In fact, we're pretty much all that's left, but we've kept fighting on. Hiding in plain sight. Doing our best to tickle their nose hairs. Granger here is a wanted woman. I'm a wanted man.

SNAPE *(dryly)*: Less wanted.

HERMIONE: To be clear: In this other world . . . ? Before you meddled?

SCORPIUS: Voldemort is dead. Killed in the Battle of Hogwarts. Harry is Head of Magical Law Enforcement. You're Minister for Magic.

HERMIONE stops, surprised by this, she looks up with a smile.

HERMIONE: I'm Minister for Magic?

RON *(wanting to join the fun)*: Brilliant. What do I do?

SCORPIUS: You run Weasleys' Wizard Wheezes.

RON: Okay, so, she's Minister for Magic and I run a—joke shop?

SCORPIUS looks at RON's hurt face.

SCORPIUS: You're mostly focused on bringing up your kids.

RON: Great. I expect their mother is hot.

SCORPIUS *(blushing)*: Well . . . Um . . . Depends what you think of . . . The thing is, you two sort of have kids—together. A daughter and a son.

The two look up, astonished.

Married. In love. Everything. You were shocked the other time too. When you were Defense Against the Dark Arts teacher and Ron was married to Padma. You're *constantly* surprised by it.

HERMIONE and RON both look at each other and then look away. And then RON looks back. RON clears his throat repeatedly. With less conviction each time.

HERMIONE: Close your mouth when you're looking at me, Weasley.

RON does so. Though he remains discombobulated.

And—Snape? What does Snape do in this other world?

SNAPE: I'm dead, presumably.

He looks at SCORPIUS, whose face drops. SNAPE smiles thinly.

You were a little too surprised to see me. How?

SCORPIUS: Bravely.

SNAPE: Who?

SCORPIUS: Voldemort.

SNAPE: How very irritating.

There's a silence as SNAPE digests.

Still, there's glory in being taken down by the Dark Lord himself, I suppose.

HERMIONE: I'm sorry, Severus.

SNAPE looks at her, and then swallows the pain. He indicates RON with a flick of his head.

SNAPE: Well, at least I'm not married to him.

HERMIONE: Which spells did you use?

SCORPIUS: Expelliarmus in the first task and Engorgio in the second.

RON: Simple Shield Charms should set both of those right.

SNAPE: And then you left?

SCORPIUS: The Time-Turner took us back, yes. That's the thing—this Time-Turner, you only get five minutes in the past.

HERMIONE: And can you still only move in time, not space?

SCORPIUS: Yes, yes, it's — uh — you travel back in the same spot you stand in —

HERMIONE: Interesting.

SNAPE and HERMIONE both know what this means.

SNAPE: Then it's just me and the boy.

HERMIONE: No offense, Snape, but I'm not trusting this to anyone, it's too important.

SNAPE: Hermione, you're the most wanted rebel in the wizarding world. Doing this will require you to go outside. When was the last time you were outside?

HERMIONE: Not for a long time, but —

SNAPE: If you're found outside, the dementors will kiss you — they'll suck out your soul.

HERMIONE: Severus, I'm done with living off scraps, making failed attempts at coups. This is our chance to reset the world.

She nods at RON, who pulls down a map.

The first task of the tournament took place at the edge of the Forbidden Forest. We turn time here, get to the tournament, block the spell, and then return safely. With precision — it can be done and it won't require us to show our faces outside in our time at all. Then we'll turn time again, make our way to the lake, and reverse the second task.

SNAPE: You're risking everything —

〜❖〜

HERMIONE: We get this right, Harry's alive, Voldemort's dead, and the Augurey is gone, for that no risk is too great. Though I am sorry what it will cost you.

SNAPE: Sometimes costs are made to be borne.

The two look at each other, SNAPE nods, HERMIONE nods back, SNAPE's face crumbles slightly.

I didn't just quote Dumbledore, did I?

HERMIONE *(with a smile)*: No, I'm pretty sure that's pure Severus Snape.

She turns to SCORPIUS, she indicates the Time-Turner.

Malfoy—

SCORPIUS brings her the Time-Turner. She smiles at it, excited to use a Time-Turner again, excited to use it for this.

Let's hope this works.

She takes the Time-Turner. It begins to vibrate, and then explodes into a storm of movement.

And there is a giant whoosh of light. A smash of noise.

And time stops. And then it turns over, thinks a bit, and begins spooling backwards, slow at first . . .

There is a bang and a flash and our gang disappear.

ACT THREE, SCENE EIGHT

EDGE OF THE FORBIDDEN FOREST,

1994

And we watch our scene from Part One replayed, but at the back of the stage rather than the front. We pick out ALBUS and SCORPIUS in their Durmstrang robes. And through it all we hear the "brilliant" (his words again, his words) LUDO BAGMAN.

SCORPIUS, HERMIONE, RON, and SNAPE watch out anxiously.

LUDO BAGMAN: And Cedric Diggory has entered the stage. And he seems ready. Scared but ready. He dodges this way. He dodges that. The girls swoon as he dives for cover. They cry as one: Don't damage our Diggory, Mr. Dragon! And Cedric skirts left and he dives right — and he readies his wand —

SNAPE: This is taking too long. The Time-Turner is spinning.

LUDO BAGMAN: What has this young, brave, handsome man got up his sleevies now?

As ALBUS attempts to summon CEDRIC's wand, HERMIONE blocks his spell. He looks at his wand — disconsolate, unsure why it hasn't worked.

❈

And then the Time-Turner spins and they look at it and panic as they're pulled into it.

A dog—he's transfigured a stone into a dog—dog diggity, Cedric Diggory—you are a doggy dynamo.

ACT THREE, SCENE NINE

EDGE OF THE FORBIDDEN FOREST

They are returned from time, at the edge of the woods, and RON is in a lot of pain. SNAPE looks around, immediately aware of the mess they're in.

RON: Ow. Ow. Owwwwwww.

HERMIONE: Ron . . . Ron . . . What has it done to you?

SNAPE: Oh no. I knew it.

SCORPIUS: The Time-Turner did something to Albus too. The first time we went back.

RON: Useful — time to — ow — tell us.

SNAPE: We're aboveground. We need to move. Now.

HERMIONE: Ron, you can still walk, come on . . .

RON does stand up, shouting in pain. SNAPE raises his wand.

SCORPIUS: Did it work?

HERMIONE: We blocked the spell. Cedric kept his wand. Yes. It worked.

SNAPE: But we came back to the wrong place—we are outside. You are outside.

RON: We need to use the Time-Turner again—get out of here—

SNAPE: We need to find shelter. We're horribly exposed.

Suddenly from around the auditorium, the feel of the breath of an icy wind.

Some black robes arise around people. Black robes that become black shapes. That become dementors.

HERMIONE: Too late.

SNAPE: This is a disaster.

HERMIONE *(she realizes what she has to do)*: They're after me, not any of you. Ron. I love you and I always have. But the three of you need to run. Go. Now.

RON: What?

SCORPIUS: What?

RON: Can we talk about the love thing first?

HERMIONE: This is still Voldemort's world. And I am done with it. Reversing the next task will change everything.

SCORPIUS: But they'll kiss you. They'll suck out your soul.

HERMIONE: And then you'll change the past. And then they won't. Go. Now.

The dementors sense them. From all sides, screaming shapes descend.

SNAPE: Go. We go.

He pulls on SCORPIUS's arm. SCORPIUS reluctantly goes with him.

HERMIONE looks at RON.

HERMIONE: You're supposed to be going too.

RON: Well, they are after me a bit and I really am in quite a lot of pain. And, you know, I'd rather be here. Expecto—

As he reaches up to cast the spell, HERMIONE stops his arm.

HERMIONE: Let's keep them here and give the boy the best chance we can.

RON looks at her and then nods sadly.

A daughter.

RON: And a son. I liked that idea too.

He looks around — he knows his fate.

I'm scared.

HERMIONE: Kiss me.

RON thinks and then does. And then the two are yanked apart. And pinned to the ground. And we watch as a golden-whitish haze is pulled from their bodies. They have their souls sucked from them. And it is terrifying.

SCORPIUS watches — helplessly.

SNAPE: Let's get down to the water. Walk. Don't run.

SNAPE looks at SCORPIUS.

Stay calm, Scorpius. They may be blind but they can sense your fear.

SCORPIUS looks at SNAPE.

SCORPIUS: They just sucked out their souls.

A dementor swoops down low over them and settles in front of SCORPIUS.

SNAPE: Think of something else, Scorpius. Occupy your thoughts.

SCORPIUS: I feel cold. I can't see. There's a fog inside me—around me.

SNAPE: You're a king, and I'm a professor. They'll only attack with good reason. Think about those you love, think about why you're doing this.

SCORPIUS: I can hear my mother. She wants me—my help—but she knows I can't—help.

SNAPE: Listen to me, Scorpius. Think about Albus. You're giving up your kingdom for Albus, right?

SCORPIUS is helpless. Consumed by all the dementor is making him feel.

One person. All it takes is one person. I couldn't save Harry for Lily. So now I give my allegiance to the cause she believed in. And it's possible—that along the way I started believing in it myself.

SCORPIUS smiles at SNAPE. He steps decisively away from the dementor.

SCORPIUS: The world changes and we change with it. I am better off in this world. But the world is not better. And I don't want that.

Suddenly DOLORES UMBRIDGE emerges in front of them.

DOLORES UMBRIDGE: Professor Snape!

SNAPE: Professor Umbridge.

DOLORES UMBRIDGE: Have you heard the news? We've caught that traitorous Mudblood Hermione Granger. She was just out here.

SNAPE: That's — fantastic.

UMBRIDGE is staring at SNAPE. He looks back.

DOLORES UMBRIDGE: With you. Granger was with you.

SNAPE: With me? You're mistaken.

DOLORES UMBRIDGE: With you and Scorpius Malfoy. A student I'm becoming increasingly concerned about.

SCORPIUS: Well . . .

SNAPE: Dolores, we're late for class, so if you'll excuse us . . .

DOLORES UMBRIDGE: If you're late for class, why are you not heading back to the school? Why are you heading to the lake?

There's a moment of pure silence. And then SNAPE does something hugely unusual — he smiles.

SNAPE: How long have you suspected?

UMBRIDGE rises off the ground. She opens her arms wide, full of Dark Magic. She takes out her wand.

DOLORES UMBRIDGE: Years. And I should have acted upon it far earlier.

SNAPE is faster with his wand.

SNAPE: Depulso!

UMBRIDGE is propelled backwards through the air.

※✦※

She always was too grand for her own good. There's no turning back now.

The sky turns even blacker still around them.

Expecto Patronum!

SNAPE sends forward a Patronus, and it's a beautiful white shape of a doe.

SCORPIUS: A doe? Lily's Patronus.

SNAPE: Strange, isn't it? What comes from within.

Dementors start to appear all around them. SNAPE knows what this means.

You need to run. I will keep them at bay for as long as I can.

SCORPIUS: Thank you for being my light in the darkness.

SNAPE looks at him, every inch a hero, he softly smiles.

SNAPE: Tell Albus—tell Albus Severus—I'm proud he carries my name. Now go. Go.

The doe looks back at SCORPIUS, and then starts to run.

SCORPIUS thinks and then runs after the doe, and around him the world gets scarier. A bloodcurdling scream goes up at one side. He sees the lake and throws himself inside.

SNAPE readies himself.

SNAPE is pulled hard to the ground and then pushed high into the air as his soul is ripped from him. As the screams just seem to multiply.

The doe turns to him with beautiful eyes, and disappears.

There is a bang and a flash. And then silence. And then there's more silence.

It's so still, it's so peaceful, it's so perfectly tranquil.

And then—SCORPIUS ascends to the surface. Breathing deeply. He looks around himself. Breathing deep, panicked breaths. He looks up at the sky. The sky certainly seems—bluer than before.

And then ALBUS ascends after him. There's a silence. SCORPIUS just looks at ALBUS, disbelieving. Both boys breathe in and out.

ALBUS: Whoa!

SCORPIUS: Albus!

ALBUS: That was close! Did you see that Merman? The guy with the—and then the thing with the—whoa!

SCORPIUS: It's you.

ALBUS: It was weird though—I thought I saw Cedric start to expand—but then he sort of started shrinking again—and I looked at you and you had your wand out . . .

SCORPIUS: You have no idea how good it is to see you again.

ALBUS: You just saw me two minutes ago.

SCORPIUS hugs ALBUS in the water, a difficult task.

SCORPIUS: A lot has happened since then.

ALBUS: Careful. You're drowning me. What are you wearing?

SCORPIUS: What am I wearing? *(He pulls off his cloak.)* What are *you* wearing? Yes! You're in Slytherin.

ALBUS: Did it work? Did we do anything?

SCORPIUS: No. And it's brilliant.

PART TWO

ALBUS looks at him—disbelieving.

ALBUS: What? We failed.

SCORPIUS: Yes. YES. AND IT'S AMAZING.

He splashes hard in the water. ALBUS pulls himself out to the bank.

ALBUS: Scorpius. Have you been eating too many sweets again?

SCORPIUS: There you go, you see—all dry humor and Albus-y. I love it.

ALBUS: Now I'm starting to get worried . . .

HARRY enters and sprints to the side of the water. Followed quickly by DRACO, GINNY, and PROFESSOR McGONAGALL.

HARRY: Albus. Albus. Are you okay?

SCORPIUS *(overjoyed)*: Harry! It's Harry Potter! And Ginny. And Professor McGonagall. And Dad. My dad. Hi. Dad.

DRACO: Hello, Scorpius.

ALBUS: You're all here.

GINNY: And Myrtle told us everything.

ALBUS: What is going on?

PROFESSOR McGONAGALL: You're the one who's just returned from time. Why don't you tell us?

SCORPIUS immediately registers what they know.

SCORPIUS: Oh no. Oh bother. Where is it?

ALBUS: Just returned from where?

SCORPIUS: I've lost it! I've lost the Time-Turner.

ALBUS *(looking at SCORPIUS, deeply annoyed)*: You've lost what?

HARRY: Time to cut the pretense, Albus.

PROFESSOR McGONAGALL: I think you've got some explaining to do.

ACT THREE, SCENE TEN

HOGWARTS, HEADMISTRESS'S OFFICE

DRACO, GINNY, and HARRY stand behind a contrite-looking SCORPIUS and ALBUS. PROFESSOR McGONAGALL is fuming.

PROFESSOR McGONAGALL: So to be clear—you illegally jumped off the Hogwarts Express, you invaded and stole from the Ministry of Magic, you took it upon yourself to change time, whereupon you disappeared two people—

ALBUS: I agree it doesn't sound good.

PROFESSOR McGONAGALL: And your response to disappearing Hugo and Rose Granger-Weasley was to go back in time again—and this time, instead of losing two people you lost a huge number of people and killed your father—and in doing so you resurrected the worst wizard the world has ever known and heralded in a new age of Dark Magic. *(Dry.)* You're correct, Mr. Potter, it doesn't sound good, does it? Are you aware how stupid you've been?

SCORPIUS: Yes, Professor.

ALBUS hesitates a moment. He looks at HARRY.

ALBUS: Yes.

HARRY: Professor, if I may —

PROFESSOR McGONAGALL: You may not. What you choose to do as parents is your matter but this is my school, and these are my students, and I will choose what punishment they will face.

DRACO: Seems fair.

HARRY looks at GINNY, who shakes her head.

PROFESSOR McGONAGALL: I should expel you but *(with a look to HARRY)* all things considered — I think it might be safer for you to remain in my care. You are in detention for — well, you can consider yourself in detention for the rest of the year. Christmas is canceled for you. You can forget visiting Hogsmeade ever again. And that's just the start . . .

Suddenly HERMIONE bursts in. All action and resolve.

HERMIONE: What did I miss?

PROFESSOR McGONAGALL *(fierce)*: It is considered polite to knock when entering a room, Hermione Granger, maybe you missed that.

HERMIONE realizes she's overstepped.

HERMIONE: Ah.

PROFESSOR McGONAGALL: If I could also give a detention to you, Minister, I would. Keeping hold of a Time-Turner, of all the stupid things!

HERMIONE: In my defense —

PROFESSOR McGONAGALL: And in a bookcase. You kept it in a bookcase. It's almost laughable.

PART TWO

⛯

HERMIONE: Minerva. *(There is an intake of breath.)* Professor McGonagall —

PROFESSOR McGONAGALL: Your children didn't exist!

HERMIONE has no reply to that.

This happened in my school, under my watch. After all that Dumbledore did, I couldn't live with myself . . .

HERMIONE: I know.

PROFESSOR McGONAGALL *(composes herself for a moment)*: Your intentions to save Cedric were honorable, if misguided. And it does sound as if you were brave, Scorpius, and you, Albus, but the lesson even your father sometimes failed to heed is that bravery doesn't forgive stupidity. Always think. Think what's possible. A world controlled by Voldemort is —

SCORPIUS: A horrific world.

PROFESSOR McGONAGALL: You are so young. *(She looks at HARRY, DRACO, GINNY, and HERMIONE.)* You're all so young. You have no idea how dark the wizarding wars got. You were — reckless — with the world some people — some very dear friends of mine and yours — sacrificed a huge amount to create and sustain.

ALBUS: Yes, Professor.

SCORPIUS: Yes, Professor.

PROFESSOR McGONAGALL: Go on. Get out. The lot of you. And find me that Time-Turner.

ACT THREE, SCENE ELEVEN

HOGWARTS, SLYTHERIN DORMITORY

ALBUS is sitting in his room. HARRY enters and looks at his son — full of anger, but cautious to not let it spill.

HARRY: Thanks for letting me come up.

ALBUS turns, he nods at his dad. He's being cautious too.

No luck, as yet, with the Time-Turner searching. They're negotiating with the Merpeople to dredge the lake.

He sits down uncomfortably.

This is a nice room.

ALBUS: Green is a soothing color, isn't it? I mean Gryffindor rooms are all well and good but the trouble with red is — it is said to send you a little mad — not that I'm casting aspersions . . .

HARRY: Can you explain why you tried to do this?

ALBUS: I thought I could — change things. I thought Cedric — it's unfair.

HARRY: Of course it's unfair, Albus, don't you think I know that? I was there. I saw him die. But to do this . . . to risk all this . . .

ALBUS: I know.

HARRY *(failing to contain his anger)*: If you were trying to do as I did, you went the wrong way about it. I didn't volunteer for adventure, I was forced into it. You did something really reckless—something really stupid and dangerous—something that could have destroyed everything—

ALBUS: I know. Okay. I know.

Pause. ALBUS wipes away a tear, HARRY notices it and takes a breath. He pulls himself back from the brink.

HARRY: Well, I was wrong too—to think Scorpius was Voldemort's son. He wasn't a black cloud.

ALBUS: No.

HARRY: And I've locked away the map. You won't see it again. Your mum left your room exactly as it was when you ran away—you know that? Wouldn't let me go in—wouldn't let anyone go in—you really scared her . . . And me.

ALBUS: Really scared you?

HARRY: Yes.

ALBUS: I thought Harry Potter wasn't afraid of anything?

HARRY: Is that how I make you feel?

ALBUS looks at his dad, trying to figure him out.

ALBUS: I don't think Scorpius said, but when we returned after failing to fix the first task, I was suddenly in Gryffindor House. Nothing was better between us then either—so—the fact that I'm in

Slytherin—that's not the reason for our problems. It's not just about that.

HARRY: No. I know. It's not just about that.

HARRY looks at ALBUS.

Are you okay, Albus?

ALBUS: No.

HARRY: No. Nor me.

꒐꒐꒐

ACT THREE, SCENE TWELVE

꒐꒐꒐

DREAM, GODRIC'S HOLLOW, GRAVEYARD

YOUNG HARRY stands looking at a gravestone covered in bunches of flowers. He has a small bunch of flowers in his hand.

AUNT PETUNIA: Go on then, lay down your grotty little flowers and then let's go. I already hate this poxy little village, I don't know why I even had the thought — Godric's Hollow, Godless Hollow, more like, the place is clearly a hive of filth — go on, chop-chop.

He approaches the grave. He stands a moment more.

Now, Harry . . . I don't have time for this. Duddy has his Cubs tonight and you know he hates to be late.

YOUNG HARRY: Aunt Petunia. We're their last living relatives, right?

AUNT PETUNIA: Yes. You and I. Yes.

YOUNG HARRY: And — they weren't popular? You said they didn't have any friends?

AUNT PETUNIA: Lily tried — bless her — she tried — it wasn't her fault, but she repelled people — by her very nature. It was her intensity, it was her manner, it was her—way. And your father—obnoxious man—extraordinarily obnoxious. No friends. Neither of them.

YOUNG HARRY: So my question is—why are there so many flowers? Why are there flowers all over their grave?

AUNT PETUNIA looks around, she sees all the flowers as if for the first time and it moves her hugely. She approaches and then sits by her sister's grave, trying hard to fight the emotions as they come to her but succumbing all the same.

AUNT PETUNIA: Oh. Yes. Well, I suppose there are a—few. Must have blown over from the other graves. Or someone's playing a trick. Yes, I think that's most likely, some young rapscallion with too much time on his hands has gone around collecting flowers from all the other graves and deposited them here—

YOUNG HARRY: But they're all marked with their names . . . "Lily and James, what you did, we will never forget," "Lily and James, your sacrifice . . ."

VOLDEMORT: I smell guilt, there is a stench of guilt upon the air.

AUNT PETUNIA *(to YOUNG HARRY)*: Get away. Get away from there.

She pulls him back. VOLDEMORT's hand rises into the air above the Potters' gravestone, the rest of him rises after. We don't see his face but his body provides a jagged, horrific shape.

I knew it. This place is dangerous. The sooner we leave Godric's Hollow the better.

YOUNG HARRY is pulled from the stage, but turns to face VOLDEMORT.

VOLDEMORT: Do you still see with my eyes, Harry Potter?

✦❖✦

YOUNG HARRY exits, disturbed, as ALBUS bursts from within VOLDEMORT's cloak. He reaches out a desperate hand towards his dad.

ALBUS: Dad . . . Dad . . .

There are some words spoken in Parseltongue.

He's coming. He's coming. He's coming.

And then a scream.

And then, right from the back of the room, whispering around everyone.

Words said with an unmistakable voice. The voice of VOLDEMORT . . .

Haaarry Pottttter.

ACT THREE,
SCENE THIRTEEN

HARRY AND GINNY POTTER'S HOUSE,
KITCHEN

HARRY is in a horrible state. Petrified by what he thinks his dreams are telling him.

GINNY: Harry? Harry? What is it? You were screaming . . .

HARRY: They haven't stopped. The dreams.

GINNY: They weren't likely to stop immediately. It's been a stressful time and—

HARRY: But I was never in Godric's Hollow with Petunia. This doesn't—

GINNY: Harry, you're really scaring me.

HARRY: He's still here, Ginny.

GINNY: Who's still here?

HARRY: Voldemort. I saw Voldemort and Albus.

GINNY: And Albus . . . ?

HARRY: He said—Voldemort said—"I smell guilt, there is a stench of guilt upon the air." He was talking to me.

HARRY looks at her. He touches his scar. Her face falls.

GINNY: Harry, is Albus still in danger?

HARRY's face grows white.

HARRY: I think we all are.

ACT THREE,
SCENE FOURTEEN

HOGWARTS, SLYTHERIN DORMITORY

SCORPIUS leans ominously over ALBUS's headboard.

SCORPIUS: Albus . . . Psst . . . Albus.

ALBUS doesn't wake.

ALBUS!

ALBUS wakes with a shock. SCORPIUS laughs.

ALBUS: Pleasant. That's a pleasant and not scary way to wake up.

SCORPIUS: You know it's the strangest of things, but ever since being in the scariest place imaginable I'm pretty much good with fear. I am — Scorpius the Dreadless. I am — Malfoy the Unanxious.

ALBUS: Good.

SCORPIUS: I mean, normally, being in lockdown, being in constant detention, it'd break me, but now — what's the worst they can do? Bring back Moldy Voldy and have him torture me? Nope.

ALBUS: You're scary when you're in a good mood, you know that?

SCORPIUS: When Rose came up to me today in Potions and called me Bread Head I almost hugged her. No, there's no almost about it, I actually tried to hug her, and then she kicked me in the shin.

ALBUS: I'm not sure being fearless is going to be good for your health.

SCORPIUS looks at ALBUS, his face grows more contemplative.

SCORPIUS: You don't know how good it is to be back here, Albus. I hated it there.

ALBUS: Apart from the Polly Chapman fancying you bits.

SCORPIUS: Cedric was a different person entirely — dark, dangerous. My dad — doing anything they wanted him to. And me? I discovered another Scorpius, you know? Entitled, angry, mean — people were frightened of me. It feels like we were all tested and we all — failed.

ALBUS: But you changed things. You had a chance and you changed time back. Changed yourself back.

SCORPIUS: Only because I knew what I should be.

ALBUS digests this.

ALBUS: Do you think I've been tested too? I have, haven't I?

SCORPIUS: No. Not yet.

ALBUS: You're wrong. The stupid thing wasn't going back once — anyone can make that mistake — the stupid thing was being arrogant enough to go back twice.

⊰⟡⊱

SCORPIUS: We both went back, Albus.

ALBUS: And why was I so determined to do this? Cedric? Really? No. I had something to prove. My dad's right—he didn't volunteer for adventure—me, this, it's all my fault—and if it wasn't for you everything could have gone Dark.

SCORPIUS: But it didn't. And you're to thank for that as much as me. When the dementors were—inside my head—Severus Snape told me to think of you. You may not have been there, Albus, but you were fighting—fighting alongside me.

ALBUS nods. Touched by this.

And saving Cedric—that wasn't such a bad idea—not in my head, anyway—though, you know, right—that we definitely can't try again.

ALBUS: Yes. I do. I do know that.

SCORPIUS: Good. Then you can help me destroy this.

SCORPIUS reveals the Time-Turner to ALBUS.

ALBUS: I'm pretty sure you told everyone that was on the bottom of a lake.

SCORPIUS: Turns out Malfoy the Unanxious is a pretty good liar.

ALBUS: Scorpius . . . We should tell someone about this . . .

SCORPIUS: Who? The Ministry kept it before, do you really trust them not to keep it again? Only you and I have experienced how dangerous this is, that means you and I have to destroy it. No one can do what we did, Albus. No one. No, *(slightly grandly)* it's time that time-turning became a thing of the past.

ALBUS: You're quite proud of that phrase, aren't you?

SCORPIUS: Been working on it all day.

ACT THREE, SCENE FIFTEEN

HOGWARTS, SLYTHERIN DORMITORY

HARRY and GINNY move quickly through the dormitory. CRAIG BOWKER JR. trails after them.

CRAIG BOWKER JR.: Can I repeat again? This is against the rules and it's the middle of the night.

HARRY: I need to find my son.

CRAIG BOWKER JR.: I know who you are, Mr. Potter, but even you must understand that it's against school covenant for parents or professors to enter a House quarters without express permission from . . .

PROFESSOR McGONAGALL charges in behind them.

PROFESSOR McGONAGALL: Please don't be tiresome, Craig.

HARRY: You got our message? Good.

CRAIG BOWKER JR. *(shocked)*: Headmistress. I'm—I was just—

HARRY pulls open a bed-curtain.

PROFESSOR McGONAGALL: He's gone?

HARRY: Yes.

PROFESSOR McGONAGALL: And young Malfoy?

GINNY pulls open another.

GINNY: Oh no.

PROFESSOR McGONAGALL: Then let's turn this school upside down. Craig, we've work to do . . .

GINNY and HARRY stay, looking at the bed.

GINNY: Haven't we been here before?

HARRY: Something feels even worse this time.

GINNY looks at her husband, full of fear.

GINNY: You spoke to him earlier?

HARRY: Yes.

GINNY: You came to his dorm and talked to him?

HARRY: You know I did.

GINNY: What did you say to our son, Harry?

HARRY can hear the accusation in her voice.

HARRY: I tried to be honest like you said—I didn't say anything.

GINNY: And you controlled yourself? How heated did it get?

HARRY: . . . I don't think I . . . You think I've scared him away again?

GINNY: I can forgive you for one mistake, Harry, maybe even two, but the more mistakes you make, the harder to forgive you it becomes.

ACT THREE, SCENE SIXTEEN

HOGWARTS, OWLERY

SCORPIUS and ALBUS emerge onto a roof bathed in silver light. There's soft hooting all around them.

SCORPIUS: So I think a simple Confringo.

ALBUS: Definitely not. For something like this you need Expulso.

SCORPIUS: Expulso? Expulso and we'll be clearing bits of Time-Turner from this owlery for days.

ALBUS: Bombarda?

SCORPIUS: And wake up everyone in Hogwarts? Maybe Stupefy. They were originally destroyed using Stupefy . . .

ALBUS: Exactly, it's been done before—let's do something new, something fun.

SCORPIUS: Fun? Look, many wizards overlook the importance of choosing the right spell, but this really matters. I think it's a much-underestimated part of modern witchcraft.

DELPHI: "A much-underestimated part of modern witchcraft"—you two are the greatest, you know that?

SCORPIUS looks up, surprised to see DELPHI has emerged behind them.

SCORPIUS: Wow. You're . . . um . . . What are you doing here?

ALBUS: It felt important to send an owl—let her know what we're doing, you know?

SCORPIUS looks at his friend accusingly.

This concerns her too.

SCORPIUS thinks, and then nods, accepting this.

DELPHI: What concerns me? What's this about?

ALBUS gets out the Time-Turner.

ALBUS: We need to destroy the Time-Turner. The things Scorpius saw after the second task . . . I'm so sorry. We can't risk going back again. We can't save your cousin.

DELPHI looks at it and then at them both.

DELPHI: Your owl said so little . . .

ALBUS: Imagine the worst possible world, and then double it. People being tortured, dementors everywhere, a despotic Voldemort, my dad dead, me never born, the world surrounded by Dark Magic—we just, we can't allow that to happen.

DELPHI hesitates. And then her face breaks.

DELPHI: Voldemort ruled? He was alive?

SCORPIUS: He ruled everything. It was terrible.

DELPHI: Because of what we did?

SCORPIUS: Humiliating Cedric turned him into a very angry young man, and then he became a Death Eater and — and — it all went wrong. Really wrong.

DELPHI looks at SCORPIUS's face carefully. Her face sinks.

DELPHI: A Death Eater?

SCORPIUS: And a murderer. He killed Professor Longbottom.

DELPHI: Then — of course — we need to destroy it.

ALBUS: You understand?

DELPHI: I'll go further than that — I'll say Cedric would have understood. We'll destroy it together, and then we'll go to my uncle. Explain the situation.

ALBUS: Thank you.

DELPHI smiles at them sadly, and then takes the Time-Turner. She looks at it and her expression changes slightly.

Oh, nice mark.

DELPHI: What?

DELPHI's cloak has loosened. An Augurey tattoo is visible on the back of her neck.

ALBUS: On your back. I hadn't noticed it before. The wings. Is that what the Muggles call a tattoo?

DELPHI: Oh. Yes. Well, it's an Augurey.

SCORPIUS: An Augurey?

DELPHI: Haven't you met them in Care of Magical Creatures? They're sinister-looking black birds that cry when rain's coming. Wizards used to believe that the Augurey's cry foretold death. When I was growing up my guardian kept one in a cage.

SCORPIUS: Your . . . guardian?

DELPHI looks at SCORPIUS, now she has the Time-Turner she's enjoying the game of this.

DELPHI: She used to say it was crying because it could see I was going to come to a sticky end. She didn't like me much. Euphemia Rowle . . . she only took me in for the gold.

ALBUS: Why would you want a tattoo of her bird, then?

DELPHI: It reminds me that the future is mine to make.

ALBUS: Cool. I might get an Augurey tattoo.

SCORPIUS: The Rowles were pretty extreme Death Eaters.

A thousand thoughts whir inside SCORPIUS's head.

ALBUS: Come on, let's get destroying . . . Confringo? Stupefy? Bombarda? Which would you use?

SCORPIUS: Give it back. Give us back the Time-Turner.

DELPHI: What?

ALBUS: Scorpius? What are you doing?

SCORPIUS: I don't believe you ever were ill. Why didn't you come to Hogwarts? Why are you here now?

DELPHI: I'm trying to bring my cousin back!

SCORPIUS: They called you the Augurey. In — the other world — they called you the Augurey.

A slow smile grows on DELPHI's face.

DELPHI: The Augurey? I rather like that.

ALBUS: Delphi?

She's too quick. Leveling her wand, she repels SCORPIUS, and she is far stronger. SCORPIUS tries to keep her back, but she quickly overpowers him.

DELPHI: Fulgari!

SCORPIUS's arms are bound in vicious, luminous cords.

SCORPIUS: Albus. Run!

ALBUS looks around, bewildered. And then starts to run.

DELPHI: Fulgari!

ALBUS is propelled to the floor, his hands tied by the same brutal binding.

And that is the first spell I've had to use on you. I thought I'd have to use plenty more. But you're far easier to control than Amos — children, particularly male children, are so naturally pliant, aren't they? Now, let's sort this mess out once and for all . . .

ALBUS: But why? But what? But who are you?

DELPHI: Albus. I am the new past.

She pulls ALBUS's wand from him and snaps it.

I am the new future.

She pulls SCORPIUS's wand from him and snaps it.

I am the answer this world has been looking for.

ACT THREE, SCENE SEVENTEEN

MINISTRY OF MAGIC, HERMIONE'S OFFICE

RON is sitting on HERMIONE's desk eating porridge.

RON: I can't get over it, really. The fact that in some realities we aren't even, you know, married.

HERMIONE: Ron, whatever this is, I've got ten minutes until the goblins show up to talk security at Gringotts—

RON: I mean, we've been together so long—and married for so long—I mean, *so* long—

HERMIONE: If this is your way of saying you want a marital break, Ron, then, to be clear, I will skewer you with this quill.

RON: Shut up. Will you shut up for once? I want to do one of those marriage renewal things I've read about. Marriage renewal. What do you think?

HERMIONE *(melting slightly)*: You want to marry me again?

RON: Well, we were only young when we did it the first time and I got very drunk and—well, to be honest, I can't remember much of it and . . . The truth is—I love you, Hermione Granger, and whatever time says—I'd like the opportunity to say so in front of lots of other people. Again. Sober.

She looks at him, she smiles, she pulls him to her, she kisses him.

HERMIONE: You're sweet.

RON: And you taste of toffee . . .

HERMIONE laughs. HARRY, GINNY, and DRACO walk in on them as they move to kiss again. They spring apart.

HERMIONE: Harry, Ginny, and—I, uh—Draco—how lovely to see you—

HARRY: The dreams. They've started again, well, they haven't stopped.

GINNY: And Albus is missing. Again.

DRACO: Scorpius too. We've had McGonagall check the entire school. They're gone.

HERMIONE: I'll get the Aurors summoned immediately, I'll—

RON: No, you won't, it's all fine. Albus—I saw him last night. It's all good.

DRACO: Where?

They all turn to look at RON, he's briefly disconcerted but batters on.

RON: I was having a couple of firewhiskies with Neville in Hogsmeade— as you do—setting the world to rights—as we do—and we were coming back—quite late, very late, and trying to work out which

Floo I could use because when you've had a drink sometimes you don't want to use the tight ones — or the turny ones or —

GINNY: Ron, if you could get to the point before we all strangle you?

RON: He hasn't run away — he's having a quiet moment — he's got himself an older girlfriend —

HARRY: An older girlfriend?

RON: And a cracking one at that — gorgeous silver hair. Saw them on the roof together, near the Owlery with Scorpius playing the gooseberry. Nice to see my love potion being used well, I thought.

HARRY has a thought.

HARRY: Her hair — was it silver and blue?

RON: That's it — silver, blue — yup.

HARRY: He's talking about Delphi Diggory. Niece of — Amos Diggory.

GINNY: This is about Cedric again?

HARRY says nothing, thinking fast. HERMIONE looks around the room, concerned, and then shouts out of the door.

HERMIONE: Ethel! Cancel the goblins.

PART TWO

✵

ACT THREE, SCENE EIGHTEEN

✵

ST. OSWALD'S HOME FOR OLD WITCHES AND WIZARDS, AMOS'S ROOM

HARRY walks in, wand outstretched, with DRACO.

HARRY: Where are they?

AMOS: Harry Potter, and what can I do for you, sir? And Draco Malfoy. I am blessed.

HARRY: I know how you've used my son.

AMOS: I've used your son? No. You, sir—you used my beautiful son.

DRACO: Tell us—now—where are Albus and Scorpius? Or face the profoundest consequences.

AMOS: But why would I know where they are?

DRACO: Don't play the senility card with us, old man. We know you've been sending him owls.

AMOS: I've done nothing of the kind.

HARRY: Amos, you're not too old for Azkaban. They were last seen on the Hogwarts tower with your niece when they disappeared.

AMOS: I have no idea what you are . . . *(He stops, a beat, confused.)* My niece?

HARRY: There are no depths to which you won't sink, are there — yes, your niece, are you denying she was there under your express instructions?

AMOS: Yes, I am — I don't have a niece.

This stops HARRY.

DRACO: Yes, you do, a nurse, works here. Your niece . . . Delphini Diggory.

AMOS: I know I don't have a niece because I never had any brothers and sisters. And nor did my wife.

DRACO: We need to find out who she is — now.

ACT THREE,
SCENE NINETEEN

HOGWARTS, QUIDDITCH PITCH

We open on DELPHI, enjoying every second of her changed identity. Where there was discomfort and insecurity, now there's just power.

ALBUS: What are we doing on the Quidditch pitch?

DELPHI says nothing.

SCORPIUS: The Triwizard Tournament. The third task. The maze. This is where the maze was. We're going back for Cedric.

DELPHI: Yes, it is time to spare the spare once and for all. We will go back for Cedric and in doing so we will resurrect the world you saw, Scorpius . . .

SCORPIUS: Hell. You want to resurrect hell?

DELPHI: I want a return to pure and strong magic. I want to rebirth the Dark.

SCORPIUS: You want Voldemort's return?

DELPHI: The one true ruler of the wizarding world. He will return. Now, you've ensured the first two tasks are a little clogged up with magic — there are at least two visits from the future in both of them and I will not risk being revealed or distracted. The third task is clean, so let's start there, shall we?

ALBUS: We won't stop him — whatever you force us to do — we know he needs to win the tournament with my dad.

DELPHI: I don't just want you to stop him. I want you to humiliate him. He needs to fly out of that maze naked on a broomstick made of purple feather dusters. Humiliation got you there before and it'll get us there again. And the prophecy will be fulfilled.

SCORPIUS: Wasn't aware that there was a prophecy, what prophecy?

DELPHI: You have seen the world as it should be, Scorpius, and today we're going to ensure its return.

ALBUS: We won't. We won't obey you. Whoever you are. Whatever you want us to do.

DELPHI: Of course you will.

ALBUS: You'll have to use Imperio. You'll have to control me.

DELPHI: No. To fulfill the prophecy, this has to be you, not a puppet of you. You have to be the one to humiliate Cedric, so Imperio just won't do — I'll have to force you by other means.

She takes out her wand. She points it at ALBUS, who sticks his chin out.

ALBUS: Do your worst.

DELPHI looks at him. And then turns her wand on SCORPIUS.

DELPHI: I will.

ALBUS: No!

DELPHI: Yes, as I thought — this seems to frighten you more.

SCORPIUS: Albus, whatever she does to me — we can't let her —

DELPHI: Crucio!

SCORPIUS yells out in pain.

ALBUS: I will . . .

DELPHI *(laughing)*: What? What on earth do you think you can do? A wizardwide disappointment? A sore on your family name? A spare? You want to stop me hurting your only friend? Then do what you're told.

She looks at ALBUS, his eyes stay resistant.

No? Crucio!

ALBUS: Stop. Please.

CRAIG runs in, full of energy.

CRAIG BOWKER JR.: Scorpius? Albus? Everyone's looking for you —

ALBUS: Craig. Get away. Get help!

CRAIG BOWKER JR.: What's happening?

DELPHI: Avada Kedavra!

DELPHI sends a blast of green light across the stage — CRAIG is propelled backwards by it — and is immediately killed.

There's a silence. A silence that seems to last for a long time.

Did you not understand? These are not childish games we are playing here. You are useful to me, your friends are not.

ALBUS and SCORPIUS look at CRAIG's body — their minds in hell.

It took me a long time to discover your weakness, Albus Potter. I thought it was pride, I thought it was the need to impress your father, but then I realized your weakness was the same as your father's: friendship. You will do exactly as you're told, otherwise Scorpius will die, just like that *spare* did.

She looks at them both.

Voldemort will return and the Augurey will sit at his side. Just as it was prophesized. "When spares are spared, when time is turned, when unseen children murder their fathers: Then will the Dark Lord return."

She smiles. She pulls SCORPIUS viciously towards her.

Cedric is the spare, and Albus —

She pulls ALBUS viciously towards her.

— the unseen child who will kill his father by rewriting time and so return the Dark Lord.

The Time-Turner starts rotating. She pulls their hands to it.

Now!

And there is a giant whoosh of light. A smash of noise.

And time stops. And then it turns over, thinks a bit, and begins spooling backwards, slow at first . . .

PART TWO

And then it speeds up.

And then there's a sucking noise. And a BANG.

ACT THREE, SCENE TWENTY

TRIWIZARD TOURNAMENT, MAZE, 1995

The maze is a spiral of hedges that don't stop moving. DELPHI walks determinedly through it. Behind her she drags ALBUS and SCORPIUS. Their arms bound, their legs reluctantly moving.

LUDO BAGMAN: Ladies and gentlemen—boys and girls—I give you—the greatest—the fabulous—the one—and the only TRIWIZARD TOURNAMENT.

There's a loud cheer. DELPHI turns left.

If you're from Hogwarts. Give me a cheer.

There's a loud cheer.

If you're from Durmstrang—give me a cheer.

There's a loud cheer.

AND IF YOU'RE FROM BEAUXBATONS GIVE ME A CHEER.

There's a fulsome cheer.

DELPHI and the boys are forced to move as a hedge closes upon them.

The French, finally showing us what they're capable of there. Ladies and gentlemen, I give you—the final of the Triwizard tasks. A maze of mysteries, a disease of uncontrollable darkness, for this maze—it lives. It lives.

VIKTOR KRUM passes across the stage, moving through the maze.

And why risk this living nightmare? Because inside this maze is a Cup—and not just any Cup—yes, the Triwizard trophy stands within this vegetation.

DELPHI: Where is he? Where is Cedric?

A hedge almost dissects ALBUS and SCORPIUS.

SCORPIUS: The hedges want to kill us too? This gets better and better.

DELPHI: You will keep up or face the consequences.

LUDO BAGMAN: The perils are plentiful, but the prizes are palpable. Who will fight their way through? Who will fall at the final hurdle? What heroes do we have within our midst? Only time will tell, ladies and gentlemen, only time will tell.

They move through the maze, SCORPIUS and ALBUS being compelled by DELPHI. As she moves ahead, the boys have a chance to talk.

SCORPIUS: Albus, we need to do something.

ALBUS: I know, but what? She has snapped our wands, we're bound, and she's threatening to kill you.

SCORPIUS: I'm ready to die if it'll stop Voldemort returning.

ALBUS: Are you?

SCORPIUS: You won't have to mourn me for long, she'll kill me and quickly kill you too.

ALBUS *(desperate)*: The flaw in the Time-Turner, the five-minute rule. We do all we can to run down the clock.

SCORPIUS: It won't work.

As another hedge changes direction, DELPHI pulls ALBUS and SCORPIUS in after her. They continue through this maze of despair.

LUDO BAGMAN: Now let me remind you of the current standings! Tied in first place — Mr. Cedric Diggory and Mr. Harry Potter. In second place — Mr. Viktor Krum! And in third place — sacré bleu, Miss Fleur Delacour.

Suddenly, ALBUS and SCORPIUS emerge from behind a hedge, they're running.

ALBUS: Where did she go?

SCORPIUS: Does it matter? Which way do you think?

DELPHI rises up after them. She's flying, and without a broom.

DELPHI: You poor creatures.

She throws the boys to the ground.

Thinking you can escape me.

ALBUS *(astonished)*: You're not — even on a broom.

DELPHI: Brooms — such unwieldy, unnecessary objects. Three minutes gone. We have two minutes left. And you will do what you're told.

SCORPIUS: No. We won't.

PART TWO

⚜

DELPHI: You think you can fight me?

SCORPIUS: No. But we can defy you. If we lay down our lives to do so.

DELPHI: The prophecy must be fulfilled. We will fulfill it.

SCORPIUS: Prophecies can be broken.

DELPHI: You're mistaken, child, prophecies are the future.

SCORPIUS: But if the prophecy is inevitable why are we here trying to influence it? Your actions contradict your thoughts—you're dragging us through this maze because you believe this prophecy needs to be enabled—and by that logic prophecies can also be broken—prevented.

DELPHI: You talk too much, child. Crucio!

SCORPIUS is racked with pain.

ALBUS: Scorpius!

SCORPIUS: You wanted a test, Albus, this is it, and we're going to pass it.

ALBUS looks at SCORPIUS, finally aware what he has to do. He nods.

DELPHI: Then you will die.

ALBUS *(full of strength)*: Yes. We will. And we'll do so gladly knowing it's stopped you.

DELPHI rises up—full of fury.

DELPHI: We don't have time for this. Cru—

MYSTERIOUS VOICE: Expelliarmus!

Bang. DELPHI's wand is pulled away from her. SCORPIUS looks on in astonishment.

Brachiabindo!

And DELPHI is bound. SCORPIUS and ALBUS then turn as one and stare in astonishment at where the bolt came from: a young, good-looking lad of seventeen or so, CEDRIC.

CEDRIC: Come no further.

SCORPIUS: But you're . . .

CEDRIC: Cedric Diggory. I heard screaming, I had to come. Name yourselves, beasts. I can fight you.

ALBUS wheels around, astonished.

ALBUS: Cedric?

SCORPIUS: You saved us.

CEDRIC: Are you also a task? An obstacle? Speak. Do I have to defeat you too?

There's a silence.

SCORPIUS: No. You just have to free us. That's the task.

CEDRIC thinks, trying to work out whether it's a trap, and then waves his wand.

CEDRIC: Emancipare! Emancipare!

The boys are freed.

And now I can go on? Finish the maze?

❦

The boys look at CEDRIC — they are heartbroken.

ALBUS: I'm afraid you have to finish the maze.

CEDRIC: Then I shall.

CEDRIC walks confidently away. ALBUS looks after him — desperate to say something, unsure what to say.

ALBUS: Cedric —

CEDRIC turns towards him.

Your dad loves you very much.

CEDRIC: What?

Behind them, DELPHI's body creeps into movement. She crawls along the ground.

ALBUS: Just thought you should know that.

CEDRIC: Okay. Um. Thank you.

CEDRIC looks at ALBUS a moment more, and then walks on. DELPHI pulls out the Time-Turner from within her robes.

SCORPIUS: Albus.

ALBUS: No. Wait . . .

SCORPIUS: The Time-Turner is spinning . . . Look at what she's doing . . . She can't leave us behind.

ALBUS and SCORPIUS both scramble to grab part of the Time-Turner.

And there is a giant whoosh of light. A smash of noise.

And time stops. And then it turns over, thinks a bit, and begins spooling backwards, slow at first . . .

And then it speeds up.

Albus . . .

ALBUS: What have we done?

SCORPIUS: We had to go with the Time-Turner, we had to try to stop her.

DELPHI: Stop me? How do you think you've stopped me? I am done with this. You may have destroyed my chances of using Cedric to darken the world but maybe you're right, Scorpius — maybe prophecies can be prevented, maybe prophecies can be broken. What is undoubtedly true is: I'm done with trying to use you annoying, incompetent creatures for anything. No more wasting precious seconds on either of you. Time to try something new.

She crushes the Time-Turner. It explodes in a thousand pieces.

DELPHI ascends again into the air. She laughs in delight as she sets off hard away.

The boys try to chase her, but they've not the slightest chance. She flies, they run.

ALBUS: No . . . No . . . You can't . . .

SCORPIUS turns back and tries to pick up the Time-Turner pieces.

The Time-Turner? It's destroyed?

SCORPIUS: Utterly. We're stuck here. In time. Wherever in time we are. Whatever it is she's planning to do.

ALBUS: Hogwarts looks the same.

SCORPIUS: Yes. And we can't be seen here. Let's get out of here before we're spotted.

ALBUS: We need to stop her, Scorpius.

SCORPIUS: I know we do — but how?

ACT THREE,
SCENE TWENTY-ONE

ST. OSWALD'S HOME FOR OLD WITCHES
AND WIZARDS, DELPHI'S ROOM

HARRY, HERMIONE, RON, DRACO, and GINNY look around a simple oak-paneled room.

HARRY: It must have been a Confundus Charm she used on him. Used on them all. She faked being a nurse, she faked being his niece.

HERMIONE: I've just checked in with the Ministry—but there's no record of her. She's a shadow.

DRACO: Specialis Revelio!

Everyone turns to look at DRACO.

Well, it was worth a try, what are you waiting for? We know nothing, so we just have to hope this room reveals something.

GINNY: Where can she have hidden anything? It's quite a spartan room.

RON: These panels, these panels must conceal something.

DRACO: Or the bed does.

DRACO starts examining the bed, GINNY a lamp, as the rest start examining the wooden wall panels.

RON *(shouting as he hammers on the walls)*: What you hiding? What you got?

HERMIONE: Maybe we should all stop for a moment and have a think about what—

GINNY unscrews a chimney from an oil lamp. There's a breathing-out noise. And then hissing words. They all turn towards it.

What was that?

HARRY: That's—I'm not supposed to be understanding—that's Parseltongue.

HERMIONE: And what does it say?

HARRY: How do I . . . ? I haven't been able to understand Parseltongue since Voldemort died.

HERMIONE: And nor has your scar hurt.

HARRY looks at HERMIONE.

HARRY: It says "Welcome, Augurey." I think I need to tell it to open . . .

DRACO: Then do it.

HARRY shuts his eyes. He speaks in Parseltongue.

The room transforms around them, becoming darker and more desperate. A writhing mass of painted snakes emerges on all the walls.

And on them, written in fluorescent paint, a prophecy.

What is this?

RON: "When spares are spared, when time is turned, when unseen children murder their fathers: Then will the Dark Lord return."

GINNY: A prophecy. A new prophecy.

HERMIONE: Cedric — Cedric was called a spare.

RON: When time is turned — she has that Time-Turner, doesn't she?

Their faces sink.

HERMIONE: She must do.

RON: But why does she need Scorpius or Albus?

HARRY: Because I'm a parent — who hasn't seen his child. Hasn't understood his child.

DRACO: Who is she? To be so obsessed with all this?

GINNY: I think I've got the answer to that.

They all turn to her. She points up . . . Their collective faces sink further and fill with fear.

Words are revealed on all the walls of the auditorium — dangerous words, horrible words.

"I will rebirth the Dark. I will bring my father back."

RON: No. She can't . . .

HERMIONE: How is it even — possible?

DRACO: Voldemort had a daughter?

They look up, terrified. GINNY takes HARRY's hand.

HARRY: No, no, no. Not that. Anything but that.

Cut to black.

ACT FOUR

ACT FOUR, SCENE ONE

❧✦❧

MINISTRY OF MAGIC,

GRAND MEETING ROOM

Wizards and witches from all over cram into the grand meeting room. HERMIONE walks onto a hastily made stage. She raises her hand for silence. Silence falls. She's surprised at the lack of effort it took. She looks around herself.

HERMIONE: Thank you. I'm so pleased so many of you were able to make my—second—Extraordinary General Meeting. I've got some things to say—I ask that we deal with questions—and there will be a lot of questions—after I speak.

As many of you know, a body has been found at Hogwarts. His name was Craig Bowker. He was a good boy. We have no firm information who was responsible for the act but yesterday we searched St. Oswald's. A room there revealed two things—one, a prophecy that promised—the return of darkness—two, written on the ceiling, a proclamation—that the Dark Lord had a—that Voldemort had a child.

The news reverberates around the room.

We don't know the full details. We're only just investigating—
questioning those with a Death Eater connection . . . And as yet no
record has been found either of the child or of the prophecy—but,
it does look like there's some truth to it. This child was kept hidden
from the wizarding world, and now she's—well now she's . . .

PROFESSOR McGONAGALL: She? A daughter? He had a daughter?

HERMIONE: Yes. A daughter.

PROFESSOR McGONAGALL: And is she now in custody?

HARRY: Professor, she did ask for no questions.

HERMIONE: It's fine, Harry. No, Professor, that's where this gets worse.
I'm afraid we've no means of taking her into custody. Or indeed,
stopping her doing anything. She's out of our reach.

PROFESSOR McGONAGALL: We can't—look for her?

HERMIONE: We have good reason to believe—she's hidden herself—
in time.

PROFESSOR McGONAGALL: Of all the reckless stupid things, you kept
the Time-Turner even now?

HERMIONE: Professor, I assure you—

PROFESSOR McGONAGALL: Shame on you, Hermione Granger.

HERMIONE flinches in the face of the anger.

HARRY: No, she doesn't deserve that. You have a right to be angry. You
all do. But this is not all Hermione's fault. We don't know how the
witch got hold of the Time-Turner. Whether my son gave it to her.

GINNY: Whether *our* son gave it her. Or whether it was stolen from him.

GINNY joins HARRY on the stage.

PROFESSOR McGONAGALL: Your solidarity is admirable, but it doesn't make your negligence negligible.

DRACO: Then it's a negligence I too should face.

DRACO walks up to the stage and stands beside GINNY. This is almost a Spartacus moment. There are gasps.

Hermione and Harry have done nothing wrong but try and protect us all. If they're guilty then I am too.

HERMIONE looks across at her cohort — moved. RON joins them on the stage.

RON: Just to say — I didn't know about much of it so can't take responsibility — and I'm pretty sure my kids had nothing to do with it — but if this lot are standing up here then so am I.

GINNY: No one can know where they are — whether they're together or apart. I trust that our sons will be doing all they can to stop her, but . . .

HERMIONE: We haven't given up. We've gone to the giants. The trolls. Everyone we can find. The Aurors are out flying, searching, talking to those who know secrets, following those who won't reveal secrets.

HARRY: But there is one truth we can't escape: That somewhere in our past a witch is trying to rewrite everything we ever knew — and all we can do is wait — wait for the moment she either succeeds or fails.

PROFESSOR McGONAGALL: And if she succeeds?

HARRY: Then—just like that—most of the people in this room will be gone. We'll no longer exist and Voldemort will rule again.

ACT FOUR, SCENE TWO

SCOTTISH HIGHLANDS,
AVIEMORE TRAIN STATION, 1981

ALBUS and SCORPIUS are looking at a STATIONMASTER, apprehensively.

ALBUS: One of us should talk to him, don't you think?

SCORPIUS: Hello, Mr. Stationmaster. Mr. Muggle. Question: Did you see a flying witch passing here? And by the way, what year is it? We just ran away from Hogwarts because we were frightened of upsetting things, but this is okay?

ALBUS: You know what annoys me most of all? Dad will think we did it deliberately.

SCORPIUS: Albus. Really? I mean, really really? We're—trapped—lost—in time—probably permanently—and you're worrying what your dad might think about it? I will never understand the two of you.

ALBUS: There's a lot to understand. Dad's pretty complicated.

SCORPIUS: And you're not? Not to question your taste in women, but you fancied . . . well . . .

They both know who he's talking about.

ALBUS: I did, didn't I? I mean, what she did to Craig . . .

SCORPIUS: Let's not think about that. Let's focus on the fact that we have no wands, no brooms, no means of returning to our time. All we have is our wits and—no, that's all, our wits—and we have to stop her.

STATIONMASTER *(in very strong Scots)*: Ye ken th' auld reekie train is running late, boys?

SCORPIUS: Sorry?

STATIONMASTER: If you're waiting oan th' auld reekie train, you'll need tae ken it's running late. Train wirks oan th' line. It's a' oan th' amended time buird.

He looks at them, they look back bewildered. He frowns and hands them an amended timetable. He points to the right bit of it.

Late.

ALBUS takes it and examines it. His face changes as he takes in enormous information. SCORPIUS just stares at the STATIONMASTER.

ALBUS: I know where she is.

SCORPIUS: You understood that?

ALBUS: Look at the date. On the timetable.

SCORPIUS leans in and reads.

SCORPIUS: The 30th October, 1981. Day before Hallows' Eve, thirty-nine years ago. But—why is she? Oh.

SCORPIUS's face falls as he realizes.

ALBUS: The death of my grandparents. The attack on my dad as a baby . . . The moment when Voldemort's curse rebounded on himself. She's not trying to bring about her prophecy—she's trying to prevent the big one.

SCORPIUS: The big one?

ALBUS: "The one with the power to vanquish the Dark Lord approaches . . ."

SCORPIUS joins in.

SCORPIUS and ALBUS: ". . . born to those who have thrice defied him, born as the seventh month dies . . ."

SCORPIUS's face falls with every word.

SCORPIUS: It's my fault. I told her that prophecies can be broken— I told her the whole logic of prophecies is questionable—

ALBUS: In twenty-four hours' time Voldemort curses himself trying to kill the baby Harry Potter. Delphi is trying to prevent that curse. She's going to kill Harry herself. We need to get to Godric's Hollow. Now.

ACT FOUR, SCENE THREE

GODRIC'S HOLLOW, 1981

ALBUS and SCORPIUS walk through the center of Godric's Hollow and it's a bustling, beautiful little village.

SCORPIUS: Well, there's no visible signs of attack that I can see . . .

ALBUS: This is Godric's Hollow?

SCORPIUS: Your dad's never taken you?

ALBUS: No, he tried to a few times but I refused.

SCORPIUS: Well, there's no time for a tour — we have a murderous witch to save the world from — but regard: The Church, St. Jerome's . . .

As he indicates a church becomes visible.

ALBUS: It's magnificent.

SCORPIUS: And St. Jerome's graveyard is supposedly magnificently haunted, *(he points in another direction)* and that's where the statue of Harry and his parents will be —

ALBUS: My dad has a statue?

SCORPIUS: Oh. Not yet. But he will. Hopefully. And this — this house is where Bathilda Bagshot lived, lives . . .

ALBUS: The Bathilda Bagshot? *A History of Magic* Bathilda Bagshot?

SCORPIUS: The very same. Oh my, that's her. Wow. Squeak. My geekness is a-quivering.

ALBUS: Scorpius!

SCORPIUS: And here it is —

ALBUS: The home of James, Lily, and Harry Potter . . .

A young, attractive couple leave a house with a baby in a pushchair. ALBUS moves towards them, SCORPIUS pulls him back.

SCORPIUS: They can't see you, Albus, it might damage time, and we're not doing that — not this time.

ALBUS: But this means, she hasn't . . . We've made it . . . She hasn't . . .

SCORPIUS: So what do we do now? Get ready to fight her? Because she's pretty . . . Fierce.

ALBUS: Yes. We haven't really thought this one through, have we? What do we do now? How do we protect my dad?

ACT FOUR, SCENE FOUR

MINISTRY OF MAGIC, HARRY'S OFFICE

HARRY is hurriedly going through paperwork.

DUMBLEDORE: Good evening, Harry.

A beat. HARRY looks up at the portrait of DUMBLEDORE, his face passive.

HARRY: Professor Dumbledore, in my office, I'm honored. I must be where the action is tonight?

DUMBLEDORE: What are you doing?

HARRY: Going through papers, seeing if I've missed anything I shouldn't have. Marshaling forces to fight in the limited way we can fight. Knowing that the battle is being raged far away from us. What else can I do?

Pause. DUMBLEDORE says nothing.

Where have you been, Dumbledore?

DUMBLEDORE: I'm here now.

HARRY: Here just as the battle is lost. Or are you denying that Voldemort is going to return.

DUMBLEDORE: It is — possible.

HARRY: Go. Leave. I don't want you here, I don't need you. You were absent every time it really counted. I fought him three times without you. I'll face him again, if needs be — alone.

DUMBLEDORE: Harry, don't you think I wanted to fight him on your behalf? I would have spared you if I could —

HARRY: "Love blinds us"? Do you even know what that means? Do you even know how bad that advice was? My son is — my son is fighting battles for us just as I had to for you. And I have proved as bad a father to him as you were to me. Leaving him in places he felt unloved — growing in him resentments he'll take years to understand —

DUMBLEDORE: If you're referring to Privet Drive, then —

HARRY: Years — *years* I spent there alone, without knowing what I was, or why I was there, without knowing that anybody cared!

DUMBLEDORE: I — did not wish to become attached to you —

HARRY: Protecting yourself, even then!

DUMBLEDORE: No. I was protecting you. I did not want to hurt you . . .

DUMBLEDORE attempts to reach out of the portrait — but he can't. He begins to cry but tries to hide it.

But I had to meet you in the end . . . eleven years old, and you were so brave. So good. You walked uncomplainingly along the path that had been laid at your feet. Of course I loved you . . . and I knew that it would happen all over again . . . that where I loved,

I would cause irreparable damage. I am no fit person to love . . . I have never loved without causing harm.

A beat.

HARRY: You would have hurt me less if you had told me this then.

DUMBLEDORE *(openly weeping now)*: I was blind. That is what love does. I couldn't see that you needed to hear that this closed-up, tricky, dangerous old man . . . loved you.

A pause. The two men are overcome with emotion.

HARRY: It isn't true that I never complained.

DUMBLEDORE: Harry, there is never a perfect answer in this messy, emotional world. Perfection is beyond the reach of humankind, beyond the reach of magic. In every shining moment of happiness is that drop of poison: the knowledge that pain will come again. Be honest to those you love, show your pain. To suffer is as human as to breathe.

HARRY: You said that to me once before.

DUMBLEDORE: It is all I have to offer you tonight.

He begins to walk away.

HARRY: Don't go!

DUMBLEDORE: Those that we love never truly leave us, Harry. There are things that death cannot touch. Paint . . . and memory . . . and love.

HARRY: I loved you too, Dumbledore.

DUMBLEDORE: I know.

He is gone. And HARRY is alone. DRACO enters.

DRACO: Did you know that in this other reality — the reality Scorpius saw into — I was Head of Magical Law Enforcement? Maybe this room will be mine soon enough. Are you okay?

HARRY is consumed in his grief.

HARRY: Come in — I'll give you the tour.

DRACO walks hesitantly inside the room. He looks around distastefully.

DRACO: The thing is, though — never really fancied being a Ministry man. Even as a child. My dad, it's all he ever wanted — me, no.

HARRY: What did you want to do?

DRACO: Quidditch. But I wasn't good enough. Mainly I wanted to be happy.

HARRY nods. DRACO looks at him a second more.

Sorry, I'm not very good at small talk, do you mind if we skip on to the serious business?

HARRY: Of course. What — serious — business?

Beat.

DRACO: Do you think Theodore Nott had the only Time-Turner?

HARRY: What?

DRACO: The Time-Turner the Ministry seized was a prototype. Made of inexpensive metal. It does the job — sure. But only being able to go back in time for five minutes — that's a serious flaw — it isn't something you'd sell to true collectors of Dark Magic.

HARRY realizes what DRACO is saying.

HARRY: He was working for you?

DRACO: No. My father. He liked owning things that no one else had. The Ministry's Time-Turners — thanks to Croaker — were always a little vanilla for him. He wanted the ability to go back further than an hour, he wanted the ability to travel back years. He'd never have used it. Secretly I think he preferred a world without Voldemort. But yes, the Time-Turner was built for him.

HARRY: And did you keep it?

DRACO reveals the Time-Turner.

DRACO: No five-minute problem, and it gleams like gold, just the way the Malfoys like it. You're smiling.

HARRY: Hermione Granger. It was the reason she kept the first, the fear that there might be a second. Hanging on to this, you could have been sent to Azkaban.

DRACO: Consider the alternative — consider if people had known that I had the ability to travel in time. Consider the rumor that would have been given increased — credence.

HARRY looks at DRACO, understanding him perfectly.

HARRY: Scorpius.

DRACO: We were capable of having children but Astoria was frail. A blood malediction, a serious one. An ancestor was cursed . . . it showed up in her. You know how these things can resurface after generations . . .

HARRY: I'm sorry, Draco.

✦

DRACO: I didn't want to risk her health, I said it didn't matter whether the Malfoy line died with me—whatever my father said. But Astoria—she didn't want a baby for the Malfoy name, for pureblood or glory, but for us. Our child, Scorpius, was born . . . it was the best day of both our lives, although it weakened Astoria considerably. We hid ourselves away, the three of us. I wanted to conserve her strength . . . and so the rumors started.

HARRY: I can't imagine what that was like.

DRACO: Astoria always knew that she was not destined for old age. She wanted me to have somebody when she left, because . . . it is exceptionally lonely, being Draco Malfoy. I will always be suspected. There is no escaping the past. I never realized, though, that by hiding him away from this gossiping, judgmental world, I ensured that my son would emerge shrouded in worse suspicion than I ever endured.

HARRY: Love blinds. We have both tried to give our sons, not what they needed, but what we needed. We've been so busy trying to rewrite our own pasts, we've blighted their present.

DRACO: Which is why you need this. I have been holding on to it, barely resisting using it, even though I would sell my soul for another minute with Astoria.

HARRY: Oh, Draco . . . we can't. We can't use it.

DRACO looks up at HARRY, and for the first time—at the bottom of this dreadful pit—they look at each other as friends.

DRACO: We have to find them—if it takes centuries, we must find our sons—

HARRY: We have no idea where they are or when they are. Searching in time when you've no idea where in time to search, that's a fool's errand. No, love won't do it and nor will a Time-Turner, I'm afraid. It's up to our sons now — they're the only ones who can save us.

ACT FOUR, SCENE FIVE

⚜

GODRIC'S HOLLOW, OUTSIDE JAMES AND LILY POTTER'S HOUSE, 1981

ALBUS: We tell my granddad and grandma?

SCORPIUS: That they'll never get to see their son grow up?

ALBUS: She's strong enough—I know she is—you saw her.

SCORPIUS: She looked wonderful, Albus. And if I were you I'd be desperate to talk to her. But she needs to be able to beg Voldemort for Harry's life, she needs to think he might die, and you're the worst spoiler in the world that didn't turn out to be true . . .

ALBUS: Dumbledore. Dumbledore's alive. We get Dumbledore involved. We do what you did with Snape—

SCORPIUS: Can we risk him knowing your dad survives? That he has kids?

ALBUS: He's Dumbledore! He can cope with anything!

SCORPIUS: Albus, there have been about a hundred books written on what Dumbledore knew, how he knew it or why he did what he did. But what's undoubtedly true—what he did—he needs to do—and I'm not going to risk messing with it. I was able to ask for help because I was in an alternate reality. We aren't. We're in the past. We can't fix time only to create more problems—if our adventures have taught us anything, they've taught us that. The dangers of talking to anyone—infecting time—are too great.

ALBUS: So we need to—talk to the future. We need to send Dad a message.

SCORPIUS: But we don't have an owl that can fly through time. And he doesn't have a Time-Turner.

ALBUS: We get a message to Dad, he'll find a way to get back here. Even if he has to build a Time-Turner himself.

SCORPIUS: We send a memory—like a Pensieve—stand over him and send a message, hope he reaches for the memory at exactly the right moment. I mean, it's unlikely, but . . . Stand over the baby—and just repeatedly shout HELP. HELP. HELP. I mean, it might traumatize the baby slightly.

ALBUS: Only slightly.

SCORPIUS: A bit of trauma now is nothing compared to what's happening . . . and maybe when he then thinks—later—he might remember the faces of us as we—shouted—

ALBUS: Help.

SCORPIUS looks at ALBUS.

SCORPIUS: You're right. It's a terrible idea.

ALBUS: It's one of your worst ideas ever.

SCORPIUS: Got it! We deliver it ourselves—we wait forty years—we deliver it—

ALBUS: Not a chance—once Delphi has set time the way she wants she'll send armies to try and find us—kill us—

SCORPIUS: So we hide in a hole?

ALBUS: As pleasurable as it will be to hide in a hole with you for the next forty years . . . they'll find us. And we'll die and time will be stuck in the wrong position. No. We need something we can control, something we know he'll get at exactly the right time. We need a—

SCORPIUS: There's nothing. Still, if I had to choose a companion to be at the return of eternal darkness with, I'd choose you.

ALBUS: No offense, but I'd choose someone massive and really good at magic.

LILY exits the house with BABY HARRY in a pram, she carefully puts a blanket on him.

His blanket. She's wrapping him in his blanket.

SCORPIUS: Well, it is a moderately cold day.

ALBUS: He always said—it's the only thing he had from her. Look at the love with which she's put it on him—I think he'd like to know about that—I wish I could tell him.

SCORPIUS: And I wish I could tell my dad—well, I'm not sure what. I think I'd like to tell him that I'm occasionally capable of more bravery than he might think I am.

ALBUS has a thought.

ALBUS: Scorpius — my dad still has that blanket.

SCORPIUS: That won't work. If we write a message on it now, even really small, he'll read it too soon. Time will be spoilt.

ALBUS: What do you know about love potions? What's the ingredient they all contain?

SCORPIUS: Amongst other things, pearl dust.

ALBUS: Pearl dust is a relatively rare ingredient, isn't it?

SCORPIUS: Mainly because it's pretty expensive. What's this about, Albus?

ALBUS: Dad and I had a fight on the day before I went to school.

SCORPIUS: This I am aware of. I believe it kind of got us into this mess.

ALBUS: I threw the blanket across the room. It collided with the love potion that Uncle Ron gave me as a joke.

SCORPIUS: He's a funny guy.

ALBUS: The potion spilt and the blanket was covered in it and I happen to know for a fact Mum hasn't let Dad touch that room since I left it.

SCORPIUS: So?

ALBUS: So it's coming up to Hallows' Eve in their time as well as ours — and he told me he always finds that blanket, he needs to be with it on Hallows' Eve — it was the last thing his mum gave him — so he will look for it and when he finds it . . .

SCORPIUS: No. Still not getting you.

ALBUS: What reacts with pearl dust?

SCORPIUS: Well, it is said that if tincture of Demiguise and pearl dust
meet . . . they burn.

ALBUS: And is tincture of *(he's unsure how to say the word)* Demiguise visible
to the naked eye?

SCORPIUS: No.

ALBUS: So if we were to get that blanket and write on it in tincture of
Demiguise, then . . .

SCORPIUS *(eureka)*: Nothing would react to it until it came into contact
with the love potion. In your room. In the present. By Dumbledore,
I love it.

ALBUS: We just need to work out where to find some . . . Demiguises.

SCORPIUS: You know, rumor has it Bathilda Bagshot never saw the
point in witches and wizards locking their doors.

The door swings open.

Rumor was right. Time to steal some wands and get potioning.

ACT FOUR, SCENE SIX

HARRY AND GINNY POTTER'S HOUSE,
ALBUS'S ROOM

HARRY is sitting on ALBUS's bed. GINNY enters. She looks at him.

GINNY: Surprised to find you here.

HARRY: Don't worry, I haven't touched anything. Your shrine is preserved. *(He winces.)* Sorry. Bad choice of words.

GINNY says nothing, HARRY looks up at her.

You know I've had some pretty terrible Hallows' Eves—but this is undoubtedly at least the—second worst.

GINNY: I was wrong—to blame you. I always accuse you of jumping to things and it was me who—Albus went missing and I assumed it was your fault. I'm sorry I did that.

HARRY: You don't think this is my fault?

GINNY: Harry, he was kidnapped by a powerful Dark witch, how can that be your fault?

HARRY: I chased him away. I chased him to her.

PART TWO

GINNY: Can we not treat this as if the battle is already lost?

GINNY nods. HARRY starts to cry.

HARRY: I'm sorry, Gin . . .

GINNY: Are you not listening to me? I'm sorry too.

HARRY: I shouldn't have survived — it was my destiny to die — even Dumbledore thought so — and yet I lived. I beat Voldemort. All these people — all these people — my parents, Fred, the Fallen Fifty — and it's me that gets to live? How is that? All this damage — and it's my fault.

GINNY: They were killed by Voldemort.

HARRY: But if I'd stopped him sooner? All that blood on my hands. And now our son has been taken too —

GINNY: He's not dead. Do you hear me, Harry? He's not dead.

She takes HARRY in her arms. There is a big pause filled with pure unhappiness.

HARRY: The Boy Who Lived. How many people have to die for the Boy Who Lived?

HARRY sways a moment, unsure. Then he notices the blanket. He walks towards it.

This blanket is all I have, you know . . . of that Hallows' Eve. This is all I have to remember them. And whilst —

He picks up the blanket. He discovers it has holes in it. He looks at it, dismayed.

This has got holes in it. Ron's idiotic love potion has burnt through it, right through it. Look at this. It's ruined. Ruined.

He opens up the blanket. He sees writing burnt through it. He's surprised.

What?

GINNY: Harry, it has — something — written —

On another part of the stage, ALBUS and SCORPIUS appear.

ALBUS: "Dad . . ."

SCORPIUS: We're starting with "Dad"?

ALBUS: So he'll know it's from me.

SCORPIUS: Harry is his name. We should start with "Harry."

ALBUS *(firm)*: We're starting with "Dad."

HARRY: "Dad," does it say, "Dad"? It's not that distinct . . .

SCORPIUS: "Dad, HELP."

GINNY: "Hello"? Does that say "Hello"? And then . . . "Good."

HARRY: "Dad Hello Good Hello"? No. This is . . . a strange joke.

ALBUS: "Dad. Help. Godric's Hollow."

GINNY: Give me that. My eyesight is better than yours. Yes. "Dad Hello Good" — that's not "Hello" again — that's "Hallow" or "Hollow"? And then some numbers — these are clearer — "3 — 1 — 1 — 0 — 8 — 1." Is this one of those Muggle telephone numbers? Or a grid reference or a . . .

HARRY looks up, several thoughts smashing through his brain at once.

HARRY: No. It's a date. 31st October, 1981. The date my parents were killed.

GINNY looks at HARRY, and then back at the blanket.

GINNY: That doesn't say "Hello." It says "Help."

HARRY: "Dad. Help. Godric's Hollow. 31/10/81." It's a message. Clever boy left me a message.

HARRY kisses GINNY hard.

GINNY: Albus wrote this?

HARRY: And he's told me where they are and when they are and now we know where she is, we know where we can fight her.

He kisses her hard again.

GINNY: We haven't got them back again yet.

HARRY: I'll send an owl to Hermione. You send one to Draco. Tell them to meet us at Godric's with the Time-Turner.

GINNY: And it is "us," okay? Don't even think about going back without me, Harry.

HARRY: Of course you're coming. We have a chance, Ginny, and by Dumbledore—that's all that we need—a chance.

ACT FOUR, SCENE SEVEN

GODRIC'S HOLLOW

RON, HERMIONE, DRACO, HARRY, and GINNY walk through a present-day Godric's Hollow. A busy market town (it's expanded over the years).

HERMIONE: Godric's Hollow. It must be twenty years . . .

GINNY: Is it just me or are there more Muggles about . . .

HERMIONE: It's become quite popular as a weekend break.

DRACO: I can see why—look at the thatched roofs. And is that a farmers' market?

HERMIONE approaches HARRY—who is looking around himself, overwhelmed by all that he's seeing.

HERMIONE: You remember when we were last here? This feels just like old times.

RON: Old times with a few unwelcome ponytails added to the mix.

DRACO knows a barb when he hears one.

DRACO: Can I just say—

RON: Malfoy, you may be all chummy chummy with Harry, and you may have produced a relatively nice child, but you've said some very unfair things to and about my wife . . .

HERMIONE: And your wife doesn't need you fighting her battles for her.

HERMIONE looks witheringly at RON. RON takes the hit.

RON: Fine. But if you say one thing about her or me . . .

DRACO: You'll do what, Weasley?

HERMIONE: He'll hug you. Because we're all on the same team, aren't we, Ron?

RON *(hesitating in the face of her unwavering gaze)*: Fine. I, um, I think you've got really nice hair. Draco.

HERMIONE: Thank you, husband. Now this seems a good spot. Let's do this.

DRACO takes out the Time-Turner—it begins spinning wildly as the others take their places around it.

And there is a giant whoosh of light. A smash of noise.

And time stops. And then it turns over, thinks a bit, and begins spooling backwards, slow at first . . .

And then it speeds up.

They look around themselves.

RON: So? Has it worked?

ACT FOUR, SCENE EIGHT

GODRIC'S HOLLOW, A SHED, 1981

ALBUS looks up, amazed to see GINNY and then HARRY, and then he takes in the rest of the happy band (RON, DRACO, and HERMIONE).

ALBUS: MUM?

HARRY: Albus Severus Potter. Are we pleased to see you.

> *ALBUS runs and throws himself into GINNY's arms. GINNY receives him, delighted.*

ALBUS: You got our note . . . ?

GINNY: We got your note.

> *SCORPIUS trots up to his dad.*

DRACO: We can hug too if you like . . .

> *SCORPIUS looks at his dad, unsure for a moment. And then they sort of half hug in a very awkward way. DRACO smiles.*

RON: Now, where's this Delphi?

SCORPIUS: You know about Delphi?

ALBUS: She's here—she's trying to kill you, we think. Before Voldemort curses himself she's going to kill you and so break the prophecy and . . .

HERMIONE: Yes, we thought that might be it too. Do you know where specifically she is now?

SCORPIUS: She's disappeared. How did you—how did you, without the Time-Turner—

HARRY *(interrupting)*: That's a long and complicated story, Scorpius. And we don't have time for it.

DRACO smiles at HARRY gratefully.

HERMIONE: Harry's right. Time is of the essence. We need to get people into position. Now, Godric's Hollow is not a large place but she could be coming from any direction. So we need somewhere that gives us good views of the town—that allows for multiple and clear observation points—and that will, most importantly, keep us hidden, because we cannot risk being seen.

They all frown, thinking.

I'd say St. Jerome's Church ticks all those boxes, wouldn't you?

ACT FOUR, SCENE NINE

GODRIC'S HOLLOW, ST. JEROME'S CHURCH, SANCTUARY, 1981

ALBUS is sleeping in a pew. GINNY watches him carefully. HARRY is looking out the opposite window.

HARRY: No. Nothing. Why isn't she here?

GINNY: We're together, your mum and dad are alive — we can turn time, Harry, we can't speed it up. She'll come when she's ready, and we'll be ready for her.

She looks at ALBUS's sleeping form.

Or some of us will be.

HARRY: Poor kid thought he had to save the world.

GINNY: Poor kid has saved the world. That blanket was masterful. I mean, he also almost destroyed the world, but probably best not to focus on that bit.

HARRY: You think he's okay?

GINNY: He's getting there, it just might take him a bit of time — and you a bit of time too.

HARRY smiles. She looks back at ALBUS. HARRY does too.

You know, after I'd opened the Chamber of Secrets — after Voldemort had bewitched me with that terrible diary and I'd almost destroyed everything —

HARRY: I remember.

GINNY: After I came out of hospital — everyone ignored me, shut me out — other than, that is, the boy who had everything — who came across the Gryffindor common room and challenged me to a game of Exploding Snap. People think they know all there is to know about you, but the best bits of you are — have always been — heroic in really quiet ways. My point is — after this is over, just remember if you could that sometimes people — but particularly children — just want someone to play Exploding Snap with.

HARRY: You think that's what we're missing — Exploding Snap?

GINNY: No. But the love I felt from you that day — I'm not sure Albus feels that.

HARRY: I'd do anything for him.

GINNY: Harry, you'd do anything for anybody. You were pretty happy to sacrifice yourself for the world. He needs to feel specific love. It'll make him stronger, and you stronger too.

HARRY: You know, it wasn't until we thought Albus had gone that I truly understood what my mother was able to do for me. A countercharm so powerful that it was able to repel the spell of death.

GINNY: And the only spell Voldemort couldn't understand—love.

HARRY: I do love him specifically, Ginny.

GINNY: I know, but he needs to feel it.

HARRY: I'm lucky to have you, aren't I?

GINNY: Extremely. And I'd be delighted to discuss just how lucky at another time. But for now—let's focus on stopping Delphi.

HARRY: We are running out of time.

A thought occurs to GINNY.

GINNY: Unless—Harry, has anyone thought—why has she picked now? Today?

HARRY: Because this is the day that everything changed . . .

GINNY: Right now you're over a year old, am I right?

HARRY: A year and three months.

GINNY: That's a year and three months she could have killed you in. Even now, she's been in Godric's Hollow for twenty-four hours. What's she waiting for?

HARRY: I'm still not entirely following—

GINNY: What if she's not waiting for you—she's waiting for him . . . to stop him.

HARRY: What?

GINNY: Delphi's picked tonight because he's here—because her father is coming. She wants to meet him. Be with him, the father she loves.

❧❖❧

Voldemort's problems started when he attacked you. If he hadn't done that . . .

HARRY: He'd have only got more powerful—the darkness would only have got darker.

GINNY: The best way to break the prophecy is not to kill Harry Potter, it's to stop Voldemort doing anything at all.

ACT FOUR, SCENE TEN

GODRIC'S HOLLOW,

ST. JEROME'S CHURCH, 1981

The group are gathered and full of confusion.

RON: So let me get this right—we're fighting to protect Voldemort?

ALBUS: Voldemort killing my grandparents. Voldemort trying to kill my dad?

HERMIONE: Of course, Ginny. Delphi's not trying to kill Harry—she's stopping Voldemort trying to kill Harry. Brilliant.

DRACO: So—we just wait? Until Voldemort turns up?

ALBUS: Does she know when he does turn up? Hasn't she come here twenty-four hours early because she isn't sure when he'll arrive and in what direction? The history books—correct me if I'm wrong, Scorpius—show nothing about when and how he arrived in Godric's Hollow?

SCORPIUS and HERMIONE: You're not wrong.

RON: Blimey! There are two of them!

❧❖❧

DRACO: So how can we use this to our advantage?

ALBUS: Do you know what I'm really good at?

HARRY: There's plenty you're good at, Albus.

ALBUS: Polyjuicing. And I think Bathilda Bagshot may have all the ingredients for Polyjuice in her basement. We can Polyjuice into Voldemort and bring her to us.

RON: To use Polyjuice you need a bit of someone. We don't have a bit of Voldemort.

HERMIONE: But I like the concept, a pretend mouse for her cat.

HARRY: How close can we get through Transfiguration?

HERMIONE: We know what he looks like. We've got some excellent wizards and witches here.

GINNY: You want to transfigure into Voldemort?

ALBUS: It's the only way.

HERMIONE: It is, isn't it?

RON steps forward bravely.

RON: Then I would like to—I think I should be him. I mean, it won't be—exactly nice being Voldemort—but without wishing to blow my own trumpet—I am probably the most chilled out of all of us and . . . so maybe transfiguring into him—into the Dark Lord—will do less damage to me than—any of you more—intense—people.

HARRY steps away, introspective.

HERMIONE: Who are you calling intense?

DRACO: I'd also like to volunteer. I think being Voldemort requires precision—no offense, Ron—and a knowledge of Dark Magic and—

HERMIONE: And I'd like to volunteer too. As Minister for Magic I think it's my responsibility and right.

SCORPIUS: Maybe we should draw lots—

DRACO: You're not volunteering, Scorpius.

ALBUS: Actually—

GINNY: No, no way. I think you're all mad. I know what that voice is like inside your head—I won't have it in mine again—

HARRY: And anyway—it has to be me.

Everyone turns to HARRY.

DRACO: What?

HARRY: For this plan to work she has to believe it's him, without hesitation. She'll use Parseltongue—and I *knew* there was a reason why I still have that ability. But more than that, I—know what it is to feel—like him. I know what it is to *be* him. It has to be me.

RON: Rubbish. Beautifully put but beautiful rubbish. No way are you going to—

HERMIONE: I'm afraid you're right, my old friend.

RON: Hermione, you're wrong, Voldemort is not something to be— Harry should not—

〜❖〜

GINNY: And I hate to agree with my brother, but—

RON: He could get stuck—as Voldemort—forever.

HERMIONE: So could any of us. Your concerns are valid, but . . .

HARRY: Hang on, Hermione. Gin.

> *GINNY and HARRY make eye contact.*

> I won't do it if you don't want me to. But it feels like the only way to me, am I wrong?

> *GINNY thinks a moment and then softly nods. HARRY's face hardens.*

GINNY: You're right.

HARRY: Then let's do this.

DRACO: Don't we need to discuss the route you're taking—the—

HARRY: She's watching for him—she'll come to me.

DRACO: And then what? When she's with you. May I remind you this is a very powerful witch.

RON: Easy. He gets her in here. We zap her together.

DRACO: "Zap her"?

> *HERMIONE looks around the room.*

HERMIONE: We'll hide behind these doors. If you can get her to this point, Harry *(she indicates the point where the light from the rose window hits the floor)*, then we come out and make sure she has no chance to escape.

RON *(with a look to DRACO)*: And then we'll *zap* her.

HERMIONE: Harry, last chance, are you sure you can do this?

HARRY: Yes, I can do this.

DRACO: No, there's too many what-ifs—too many things that can go wrong—the Transfiguration could not hold, she could see through it—if she escapes us now there's no telling the damage she can do—we need time to properly plan, to—

ALBUS: Draco, trust my dad. He won't let us down.

HARRY looks at ALBUS—moved.

HERMIONE: Wands.

Everyone withdraws their wands. HARRY clasps his.

There's a light that builds—that overwhelms . . .

The Transfiguration is slow and monstrous.

And the form of VOLDEMORT emerges from HARRY.

And it's horrendous.

He turns.

He looks around at his friends and family.

They look back—aghast.

RON: Bloody hell.

HARRY/VOLDEMORT: It worked, then?

GINNY *(gravely)*: Yes. It worked.

ACT FOUR, SCENE ELEVEN

GODRIC'S HOLLOW,
ST. JEROME'S CHURCH, 1981

RON, HERMIONE, DRACO, SCORPIUS, and ALBUS stand at the window, looking out. GINNY can't look. She sits further back.

ALBUS notices his mum sitting apart. He walks over to her.

ALBUS: It's going to be okay, you know that, Mum?

GINNY: I know it is. Or I hope I do. I just—don't want to see him like that. The man I love shrouded in the man I hate.

ALBUS sits beside his mum.

ALBUS: I liked her, Mum, you know that? I really liked her. Delphi. And she was—Voldemort's daughter?

GINNY: That's what they're good at, Albus—catching innocents in their web.

ALBUS: This is all my fault.

GINNY takes ALBUS in her arms.

GINNY: How funny. Your dad seems to think it's all his. Strange pair that you are.

SCORPIUS: That's her. That's her. She's seen him.

HERMIONE: Positions. Everybody. And remember, don't come out until he's got her in the light—we've one shot at this, we don't want to mess it up.

They all move fast.

DRACO: Hermione Granger, I'm being bossed around by Hermione Granger. *(She turns towards him. He smiles.)* And I'm mildly enjoying it.

SCORPIUS: Dad . . .

They scatter. They hide behind two major doors.

HARRY/VOLDEMORT reenters the church. He walks a few paces and then he turns.

HARRY/VOLDEMORT: Whichever witch or wizard is following me, I assure you, you will regret it.

DELPHI emerges behind him. She is compelled to him. This is her father and this is the moment she's waited for her entire life.

DELPHI: Lord Voldemort. It is me. I am following you.

HARRY/VOLDEMORT: I do not know you. Leave me.

She breathes deeply.

DELPHI: I am your daughter.

HARRY/VOLDEMORT: If you were my daughter, I'd know of you.

DELPHI looks at him imploringly.

DELPHI: I am from the future. The child of Bellatrix Lestrange and you. I was born in Malfoy Manor before the Battle of Hogwarts. A battle you are going to lose. I have come to save you.

HARRY/VOLDEMORT turns. She meets his eyes.

It was Rodolphus Lestrange, Bellatrix's loyal husband, who on return from Azkaban told me who I was and revealed the prophecy he thought I was destined to fulfill. I am your daughter, sir.

HARRY/VOLDEMORT: I am familiar with Bellatrix and there are certain similarities in your face — though you haven't inherited the best of her. But without proof . . .

DELPHI speaks intently in Parseltongue.

HARRY/VOLDEMORT laughs viciously.

That's your proof?

DELPHI effortlessly rises into the air. HARRY/VOLDEMORT steps back — amazed.

DELPHI: I am the Augurey to your Dark Lord, and I am ready to give all that I have to serve you.

HARRY/VOLDEMORT *(trying not to show his shock)*: You learnt — flight — from — me?

DELPHI: I have tried to follow the path you set.

HARRY/VOLDEMORT: I have never met a witch or a wizard who's attempted to be my equal before.

DELPHI: Do not mistake — I would not claim to be worthy of you, Lord. But I have devoted my life to being a child you could be proud of.

HARRY/VOLDEMORT *(interrupting)*: I see what you are, and I see what you could be. Daughter.

She looks at him, desperately moved.

DELPHI: Father?

HARRY/VOLDEMORT: Together, the power we could wield.

DELPHI: Father . . .

HARRY/VOLDEMORT: Come here, in the light, so I may examine what my blood made.

DELPHI: Your mission is a mistake. Attacking Harry Potter is a mistake. He will destroy you.

HARRY/VOLDEMORT's hand turns into HARRY's hand. He looks at it, astonished and dismayed, and then quickly pulls it inside his sleeve.

HARRY/VOLDEMORT: He is a baby.

DELPHI: He has his mother's love. Your spell will rebound, destroying you and making him too powerful and you too weak. You will recover to spend the next seventeen years consumed in a battle with him — a battle you will lose.

HARRY/VOLDEMORT's hair begins to sprout, he feels it, he attempts to cover it. He pulls his hood over his head.

HARRY/VOLDEMORT: Then I won't attack him. You are right.

DELPHI: Father?

HARRY/VOLDEMORT shrinks down — he is now more HARRY than VOLDEMORT. He turns his back to DELPHI.

Father?

HARRY *(trying desperately to still sound like VOLDEMORT)*: Your plan is a good one. The fight is off. You have served me well, now come here into the light so I may examine you.

DELPHI sees a door slightly sway open and then be pulled shut. She frowns at it, thinking rapidly, her suspicion growing.

DELPHI: Father . . .

She tries to get a glimpse of his face again — there is almost a dance happening here.

You are not Lord Voldemort.

DELPHI unleashes a bolt from her hand. HARRY matches her.

Incendio!

HARRY: Incendio!

The bolts meet in a beautiful explosion in the middle of the room.

And with her other hand DELPHI sends bolts to both doors as they try to open them.

DELPHI: Potter. Colloportus!

HARRY looks at the doors, dismayed.

What? Thought your friends were going to join you, did you?

HERMIONE *(from off)*: Harry . . . Harry . . .

GINNY *(from off)*: She's sealed the doors from your side.

HARRY: Fine. I'll deal with you alone.

He moves to attack her again. But she is far stronger. HARRY's wand ascends upwards towards her. He is disarmed. He is helpless.

How did you . . . ? What are you?

DELPHI: I've watched you for a long time, Harry Potter. I know you better than my father did.

HARRY: You think you've learnt my weaknesses?

DELPHI: I've studied to be worthy of him! Yes, even though he is the supreme wizard of all time, he will be proud of me. Expulso!

HARRY rolls away as the floor explodes behind him. He crawls frantically under a church pew, trying to work out how he can fight her.

Are you crawling away from me? Harry Potter. Hero of the wizarding world. Crawling away like a rat. Wingardium Leviosa!

The church pew ascends into the air.

The question is whether it's worth my time to kill you — knowing that as soon as I stop my father your destruction will be assured. How to decide? Oh, I'm bored, I'll kill you.

She sends the pew down hard upon him. It smashes as he rolls desperately away.

ALBUS emerges from a grate on the floor. Neither notice.

Avada —

ALBUS: Dad . . .

HARRY: Albus! No!

DELPHI: Two of you? Choices, choices. I think I'll kill the boy first. Avada Kedavra!

She fires the Killing Curse at ALBUS — but HARRY throws him out of the way. The bolt smashes into the ground.

He fires a bolt back.

You think you're stronger than me?

HARRY: No. I'm not.

They fire bolts mercilessly at each other as ALBUS rolls quickly away and slams a spell into one door and then another.

But we are.

ALBUS opens both doors with his wand.

ALBUS: Alohomora! Alohomora!

HARRY: I've never fought alone, you see. And I never will.

And HERMIONE, RON, GINNY, and DRACO emerge from the doors, and fire up their spells at DELPHI, who screams out in exasperation. This is titanic. But she can't fight them all.

There are a series of bangs — and then, overwhelmed, DELPHI tumbles to the floor.

DELPHI: No . . . No . . .

HERMIONE: Brachiabindo!

She's bound.

HARRY advances towards DELPHI. He doesn't take his eyes off her. All the others stay back.

HARRY: Albus, are you okay?

ALBUS: Yes, Dad, I'm okay.

HARRY still doesn't take his eyes off DELPHI. He's still scared of her.

HARRY: Ginny, has he been injured? I need to know he's safe . . .

GINNY: He insisted. He was the only one small enough to crawl through the grate. I tried to stop him.

HARRY: Just tell me he's okay.

ALBUS: I'm fine, Dad. I promise.

HARRY keeps advancing towards DELPHI.

HARRY: A lot of people have tried to hurt me — but my son! You dare hurt my son!

DELPHI: I only wanted to know my father.

These words take HARRY by surprise.

HARRY: You can't remake your life. You'll always be an orphan. That never leaves you.

DELPHI: Just let me — see him.

HARRY: I can't and I won't.

DELPHI *(truly pitiful)*: Then kill me.

HARRY thinks a moment.

HARRY: I can't do that either.

ALBUS: What? Dad? She's dangerous.

HARRY: No, Albus . . .

ALBUS: But she's a murderer—I've seen her murder—

HARRY turns and looks at his son and then at GINNY.

HARRY: Yes. Albus, she's a murderer, and we're not.

HERMIONE: We have to be better than them.

RON: Yeah, it's annoying but it's what we learnt.

DELPHI: Take my mind. Take my memory. Make me forget who I am.

RON: No. We'll take you back to our time.

HERMIONE: And you'll go to Azkaban. Same as your mother.

DRACO: Where you'll rot.

HARRY hears a noise. A hissing noise.

And then there is a noise like death—a noise like nothing else we've heard before.

Haaarry Pottttter . . .

SCORPIUS: What's that?

HARRY: No. No. Not yet.

ALBUS: What?

RON: Voldemort.

DELPHI: Father?

HERMIONE: Now? Here?

DELPHI: Father!

DRACO: Silencio! *(DELPHI is gagged.)* Wingardium Leviosa! *(She is sent upwards and away.)*

HARRY: He's coming. He's coming right now.

VOLDEMORT comes through the back of the stage, and across it, and walks down into the auditorium. He brings death with him. And everyone knows it.

❧✦❧

ACT FOUR, SCENE TWELVE

❧✦❧

GODRIC'S HOLLOW, 1981

HARRY looks after VOLDEMORT helplessly.

HARRY: Voldemort is going to kill my mum and dad—and there's nothing I can do to stop him.

DRACO: That's not true.

SCORPIUS: Dad, now is not the time . . .

ALBUS: There is something you could do—to stop him. But you won't.

DRACO: That's heroic.

GINNY takes HARRY's hand.

GINNY: You don't have to watch, Harry. We can go home.

HARRY: I'm letting it happen . . . Of course I have to watch.

HERMIONE: Then we'll all witness it.

RON: We'll all watch.

We hear unfamiliar voices . . .

JAMES *(from off)*: Lily, take Harry and go! It's him! Go! Run! I'll hold him off . . .

There is a blast, and then a laugh.

You keep away, you understand—you keep away.

VOLDEMORT *(from off)*: Avada Kedavra!

HARRY flinches as green light flashes around the auditorium.

ALBUS takes his hand. HARRY grasps hold of it. He needs it.

ALBUS: He did everything he could.

GINNY rises beside him and takes HARRY's other hand. He leans into them, they're holding him up now.

HARRY: That's my mum, at the window. I can see my mother, she looks beautiful.

There's the sound of banging as doors are blasted off.

LILY *(from off)*: Not Harry, not Harry, please not Harry . . .

VOLDEMORT *(from off)*: Stand aside, you silly girl . . . Stand aside, now . . .

LILY *(from off)*: Not Harry, please no, take me, kill me instead . . .

VOLDEMORT *(from off)*: This is my last warning—

LILY *(from off)*: Not Harry! Please . . . Have mercy . . . have mercy . . . Not my son! Please—I'll do anything.

VOLDEMORT *(from off)*: Avada Kedavra!

PART TWO

And it's like lightning passes through HARRY's body. He's sent to the floor, a pure mess of grief.

And a noise like a shrunken scream descends and ascends around us.

And we just watch.

And slowly what was there is no longer there.

And the stage transforms and rotates.

And HARRY and his family and his friends are rotated off and away.

ACT FOUR, SCENE THIRTEEN

GODRIC'S HOLLOW, INSIDE JAMES AND LILY POTTER'S HOUSE, 1981

And we're in the ruins of a house. A house that has undergone a vicious attack.

HAGRID walks through the ruins.

HAGRID: James?

> *He looks about himself.*
>
> Lily?
>
> *He walks slowly, unwilling to see too much too soon. He is entirely overwhelmed.*
>
> *And then he sees them, and he stops, and he says nothing.*
>
> Oh. Oh. That's not — that's not — I weren't — They told me, but — I were hoping for better . . .
>
> *He looks at them and bows his head. He mutters a few words, and then he takes some crumpled flowers from his deep pockets and lays them on the floor.*
>
> I'm sorry, they told me, he told me, Dumbledore told me, I can't wait with yeh. Them Muggles are coming, yeh see, with their

flashing blues and they won't 'preciate a big lummox like me, would they?

He lets out a sob.

Hard though it is to leave yeh.

I want yeh to know—yeh won't be forgotten—not by me—not by anyfolk.

And then he hears a sound—the sound of a baby snuffling. HAGRID turns towards it, walking with more intensity now.

He looks down and stands over the crib. Which seems to radiate light.

Well. Hello. Yeh must be Harry.
Hello, Harry Potter.
I'm Rubeus Hagrid.
And I'm gonna be yer friend whether yeh like it or not.
'Cos yeh've had it tough, not that yeh know it yet.
An' yer gonna need friends.
Now yeh best come with me, don't yeh think?

As flashing blue lights fill the room giving it an almost ethereal glow—he lifts BABY HARRY gently into his arms.

And then—without looking back—he strides away through the house.

And we descend into soft black.

ACT FOUR, SCENE FOURTEEN

HOGWARTS, CLASSROOM

SCORPIUS and ALBUS run into a room, full of excitement. They slam the door after themselves.

SCORPIUS: I can't quite believe I did that.

ALBUS: I can't quite believe you did that either.

SCORPIUS: Rose Granger-Weasley. I asked out Rose Granger-Weasley.

ALBUS: And she said no.

SCORPIUS: But I asked her. I planted the acorn. The acorn that will grow into our eventual marriage.

ALBUS: You are aware that you're an utter fantasist.

SCORPIUS: And I'd agree with you — only Polly Chapman did ask me to the school ball . . .

ALBUS: In an alternate reality where you were significantly — really significantly more popular — a different girl asked you out — and that means —

SCORPIUS: And yes, logic would dictate I should be pursuing Polly—or allowing her to pursue me—she's a notorious beauty, after all—but a Rose is a Rose.

ALBUS: You know logic would dictate that you're a freak? Rose hates you.

SCORPIUS: Correction, she used to hate me, but did you see the look in her eyes when I asked? That wasn't hate, that was pity.

ALBUS: And pity's good?

SCORPIUS: Pity is a start, my friend, a foundation on which to build a palace—a palace of love.

ALBUS: I honestly thought I'd be the first of us to get a girlfriend.

SCORPIUS: Oh, you will, undoubtedly, probably that new smoky-eyed Potions professor—she's old enough for you, right?

ALBUS: I don't have a thing about older women!

SCORPIUS: And you've got time—a lot of time—to seduce her. Because Rose is going to take years to persuade.

ALBUS: I admire your confidence.

ROSE comes past them on the stairs. She looks at them both.

ROSE: Hi.

Neither boy knows quite how to reply—she looks at SCORPIUS.

This is only going to be weird if you let it be weird.

SCORPIUS: Received and entirely understood.

ROSE: Okay. "Scorpion King."

She walks off with a smile on her face. SCORPIUS and ALBUS look at each other. ALBUS grins and punches SCORPIUS on the arm.

ALBUS: Maybe you're right—pity is a start.

SCORPIUS: Are you heading to Quidditch? Slytherin are playing Hufflepuff—it's a big one—

ALBUS: I thought we hated Quidditch?

SCORPIUS: People can change. Besides, I've been practicing. I think I might make the team eventually. Come on.

ALBUS: I can't. My dad's arranged to come up—

SCORPIUS: He's taking time away from the Ministry?

ALBUS: He wants to go on a walk—something to show me—share with me—something.

SCORPIUS: A walk?

ALBUS: I know, I think it's a bonding thing or something similarly vomit-inducing. Still, you know, I think I'll go.

SCORPIUS reaches in and hugs ALBUS.

What's this? I thought we decided we don't hug.

SCORPIUS: I wasn't sure. Whether we should. In this new version of us—I had in my head.

ALBUS: Better ask Rose if it's the right thing to do.

SCORPIUS: Ha! Yeah. Right.

The two boys dislocate and grin at each other.

ALBUS: I'll see you at dinner.

ACT FOUR, SCENE FIFTEEN

A BEAUTIFUL HILL

HARRY and ALBUS walk up a hill on a beautiful summer's day. They say nothing, enjoying the sun on their faces as they climb.

HARRY: So are you ready?

ALBUS: For what?

HARRY: Well, there's the fourth-year exams — and then the fifth year — big year — in my fifth year I did —

He looks at ALBUS. He smiles. He talks quickly.

I did a lot of stuff. Some of it good. Some of it bad. A lot of it quite confusing.

ALBUS: Good to know.

HARRY smiles.

I got to watch them — you know — for a bit — your mum and dad. They were — you had fun together. Your dad used to love to do this smoke ring thing with you where you . . . well, you couldn't stop giggling.

HARRY: Yes?

ALBUS: I think you'd have liked them. And I think me, Lily, and James would have liked them too.

HARRY nods. There's a slightly uncomfortable silence. Both are trying to reach each other here, both are failing.

HARRY: You know, I thought I'd lost him—Voldemort—I thought I'd lost him—and then my scar started hurting again and I had dreams of him and I could even speak Parseltongue again and I started to feel like I'd not changed at all—that he'd never let me go—

ALBUS: And had he?

HARRY: The part of me that was Voldemort died a long time ago, but it wasn't enough to be physically rid of him—I had to be mentally rid of him. And that—is a lot to learn for a forty-year-old man.

He looks at ALBUS.

That thing I said to you—it was unforgivable, and I can't ask you to forget it but I can hope we move past it. I'm going to try to be a better dad for you, Albus. I am going to try and—be honest with you and . . .

ALBUS: Dad, you don't need to—

HARRY: You told me you don't think I'm scared of anything, and that—I mean, I'm scared of everything. I mean, I'm afraid of the dark, did you know that?

ALBUS: Harry Potter is afraid of the dark?

HARRY: I don't like small spaces and—I've never told anyone this, but I don't much like—*(he hesitates before saying it)* pigeons.

ALBUS: You don't like pigeons?

HARRY *(he scrunches up his face)*: Nasty, pecky, dirty things. They give me the creeps.

ALBUS: But pigeons are harmless!

HARRY: I know. But the thing that scares me most, Albus Severus Potter, is being a dad to you. Because I'm operating without wires here. Most people at least have a dad to base themselves on—and either try to be or try not to be. I've got nothing—or very little. So I'm learning, okay? And I'm going to try with everything I've got—to be a good dad for you.

ALBUS: And I'll try and be a better son. I know I'm not James, Dad, I'll never be like you two—

HARRY: James is nothing like me.

ALBUS: Isn't he?

HARRY: Everything comes easy for James. My childhood was a constant struggle.

ALBUS: So was mine. So you're saying—am I—like you?

HARRY smiles at ALBUS.

HARRY: Actually you're more like your mum—bold, fierce, funny—which I like—which I think makes you a pretty great son.

ALBUS: I almost destroyed the world.

HARRY: Delphi wasn't going anywhere, Albus—you brought her out into the light and you found a way for us to fight her. You may not see it now, but you saved us.

ALBUS: But shouldn't I have done better?

HARRY: You don't think I ask myself the same questions?

ALBUS (*stomach sinking further, he knows this is not what his dad would do*): And then—when we caught her—I wanted to kill her.

HARRY: You'd watched her murder Craig, you were angry, Albus, and that's okay. And you wouldn't have done it.

ALBUS: How do you know that? Maybe that's my Slytherin side. Maybe that's what the Sorting Hat saw in me.

HARRY: I don't understand your head, Albus—actually, you know what, you're a teenager, I shouldn't be able to understand your head, but I do understand your heart. I didn't—for a long time—but thanks to this—"escapade"—I know what you got in there. Slytherin, Gryffindor, whatever label you've been given—I know—*know*—that heart is a good one—yeah, whether you like it or not, you're on your way to being some wizard.

ALBUS: Oh I'm not going to be a wizard, I'm going into pigeon racing. I'm quite excited about it.

HARRY grins.

HARRY: Those names you have—they shouldn't be a burden. Albus Dumbledore had his trials too, you know—and Severus Snape, well, you know all about him—

ALBUS: They were good men.

HARRY: They were great men, with huge flaws, and you know what—those flaws almost made them greater.

ALBUS looks around himself.

ALBUS: Dad? Why are we here?

HARRY: This is where I often come.

ALBUS: But this is a graveyard . . .

HARRY: And here is Cedric's grave.

ALBUS: Dad?

HARRY: The boy who was killed—Craig Bowker—how well did you know him?

ALBUS: Not well enough.

HARRY: I didn't know Cedric well enough either. He could have played Quidditch for England. Or been a brilliant Auror. He could have been anything. And Amos is right—he was stolen. So I come here. Just to say sorry. When I can.

ALBUS: That's a—good thing to do.

ALBUS joins his dad in front of CEDRIC's grave. HARRY smiles at his son and looks up at the sky.

HARRY: I think it's going to be a nice day.

He touches his son's shoulder. And the two of them—just slightly—melt together.

ALBUS (*smiles*): So do I.

The End

ABOUT THE PRODUCTION

Harry Potter and the Cursed Child Parts One and Two was first produced by Sonia Friedman Productions, Colin Callender, and Harry Potter Theatrical Productions. It premiered at the Palace Theatre in London, England, on July 30, 2016, with the following cast (in alphabetical order):

CRAIG BOWKER JR. . . . . Jeremy Ang Jones

MOANING MYRTLE, LILY POTTER SR. . . . . .Annabel Baldwin

UNCLE VERNON, SEVERUS SNAPE, LORD VOLDEMORT . . . . . Paul Bentall

SCORPIUS MALFOY . . . . .Anthony Boyle

ALBUS POTTER . . . . .Sam Clemmett

HERMIONE GRANGER . . . . Noma Dumezweni

POLLY CHAPMAN . . . . Claudia Grant

HAGRID, SORTING HAT . . . . .Chris Jarman

YANN FREDERICKS . . . . .James Le Lacheur

AUNT PETUNIA, MADAM HOOCH,

    DOLORES UMBRIDGE . . . . Helena Lymbery

AMOS DIGGORY, ALBUS DUMBLEDORE . . . . Barry McCarthy

TROLLEY WITCH, PROFESSOR McGONAGALL . . . . Sandy McDade

STATIONMASTER . . . . Adam McNamara

GINNY POTTER . . . . Poppy Miller

CEDRIC DIGGORY, JAMES POTTER JR.,

    JAMES POTTER SR. . . . . .Tom Milligan

DUDLEY DURSLEY, KARL JENKINS, VIKTOR KRUM . . . . .Jack North

HARRY POTTER . . . . Jamie Parker

DRACO MALFOY . . . . Alex Price

BANE . . . . Nuno Silva

ROSE GRANGER-WEASLEY, YOUNG HERMIONE . . . . . . Cherrelle Skeete

DELPHI DIGGORY . . . . Esther Smith

RON WEASLEY . . . . Paul Thornley

YOUNG HARRY POTTER . . . . Rudi Goodman, Alfred Jones,

    Bili Keogh, Ewan Rutherford, Nathaniel Smith, Dylan Standen

LILY POTTER JR. . . . Zoe Brough, Cristina Fray, Christiana Hutchings

OTHER ROLES PLAYED BY . . . . Nicola Alexis, Jeremy Ang Jones,

    Rosemary Annabella, Jack Bennett, Paul Bentall, Morag Cross,

    Claudia Grant, James Howard, Lowri James, Chris Jarman,

    Martin Johnston, James Le Lacheur, Helena Lymbery,

    Barry McCarthy, Andrew McDonald, Adam McNamara,

    Tom Milligan, Jack North, Stuart Ramsey, Nuno Silva,

    Cherrelle Skeete

SWINGS. . . . . Helen Aluko, Morag Cross, Chipo Kureya,

    Tom Mackley, Joshua Wyatt

ABOUT THE PRODUCTION

MOVEMENT CAPTAIN . . . . Nuno Silva

ASSISTANT MOVEMENT CAPTAIN . . . . Jack North

VOICE CAPTAIN . . . . Morag Cross

ABOUT THE PRODUCTION

PRODUCTION CREDITS

ORIGINAL STORY . . . . J.K. Rowling, John Tiffany, Jack Thorne

PLAYWRIGHT . . . . .Jack Thorne

DIRECTOR . . . . .John Tiffany

MOVEMENT DIRECTOR . . . . .Steven Hoggett

SET DESIGNER . . . . .Christine Jones

COSTUME DESIGNER . . . . Katrina Lindsay

COMPOSER & ARRANGER . . . . .Imogen Heap

LIGHTING DESIGNER . . . . .Neil Austin

SOUND DESIGNER . . . . Gareth Fry

ILLUSIONS & MAGIC . . . . Jamie Harrison

MUSIC SUPERVISOR & ARRANGER . . . . Martin Lowe

CASTING DIRECTOR . . . . Julia Horan CDG

PRODUCTION MANAGER . . . . Gary Beestone

PRODUCTION STAGE MANAGER . . . . Sam Hunter

ASSOCIATE DIRECTOR . . . . Des Kennedy

ASSOCIATE MOVEMENT DIRECTOR . . . . .Neil Bettles

ASSOCIATE SET DESIGNER . . . . Brett J. Banakis

ASSOCIATE SOUND DESIGNER . . . . Pete Malkin

ILLUSIONS & MAGIC ASSOCIATE . . . . Chris Fisher

CASTING ASSOCIATE . . . . Lotte Hines

ASSISTANT LIGHTING DESIGNER . . . . Adam King

CostUME DESIGN SUPERVISOR . . . . Sabine Lemaître

HAIR, WIGS & MAKE-UP . . . . Carole Hancock

PROPS SUPERVISORS . . . . Lisa Buckley, Mary Halliday

MUSIC EDITOR . . . . Phij Adams

MUSIC PRODUCTION . . . . Imogen Heap

SPECIAL EFFECTS . . . . Jeremy Chernick

VIDEO DESIGN . . . . Finn Ross, Ash Woodward

DIALECT COACH . . . . Daniele Lydon

VOICE COACH . . . . Richard Ryder

COMPANY STAGE MANAGER . . . . Richard Clayton

STAGE MANAGER . . . . Jordan Noble-Davies

DEPUTY STAGE MANAGER . . . . Jenefer Tait

ASSISTANT STAGE MANAGERS . . . . Oliver Bagwell Purefoy,
    Tom Gilding, Sally Inch, Ben Sherratt

RESIDENT DIRECTOR . . . . Pip Minnithorpe

HEAD OF WARDROBE . . . . Amy Gillot

DEPUTY HEAD OF WARDROBE . . . . Laura Watkins

WARDROBE ASSISTANTS . . . . Kate Anderson, Leanne Hired

DRESSERS . . . . George Amielle, Melissa Cooke, Rosie Etheridge,
    John Ovenden, Emilee Swift

HEAD OF HAIR, WIGS & MAKE-UP . . . . Nina Van Houten

DEPUTY HEAD OF HAIR, WIGS & MAKE-UP . . . . Alice Townes

HAIR, WIGS & MAKE-UP ASSISTANTS . . . . Charlotte Briscoe,
    Jacob Fessey, Cassie Murphie

ABOUT THE PRODUCTION

HEAD OF SOUND . . . . Chris Reid

DEPUTY HEAD OF SOUND . . . . .Rowena Edwards

SOUND NO. 3 . . . . Laura Caplin

SFX OPERATOR. . . . . Callum Donaldson

HEAD OF AUTOMATION . . . . .Josh Peters

DEPUTY HEAD OF AUTOMATION . . . . .Jamie Lawrence

AUTOMATION NO. 3 . . . . Jamie Robson

SHOW CHIEF LX . . . . David Treanor

PERFORMER FLYING TECHNICIAN . . . . .Paul Gurney

CHAPERONES . . . . David Russell, Eleanor Dowling

GENERAL MANAGEMENT . . . . .Sonia Friedman Productions

EXECUTIVE DIRECTOR . . . . .Diane Benjamin

EXECUTIVE PRODUCER. . . . . Pam Skinner

ASSOCIATE PRODUCER . . . . .Fiona Stewart

ASSISTANT PRODUCER . . . . Ben Canning

GENERAL MANAGEMENT ASSISTANT . . . . Max Bittleston

PRODUCTION ASSISTANT . . . . Imogen Clare-Wood

MARKETING MANAGER . . . . Laura Jane Elliott

REVENUE MANAGER. . . . . .Mark Payn

ASSOCIATE PRODUCER (DEVELOPMENT) . . . . .Lucie Lovatt

DEVELOPMENT ASSISTANT . . . . Lydia Rynne

LITERARY ASSOCIATE . . . . Jack Bradley

OFFICE ASSISTANT . . . . .Jordan Eaton

HOUSE SEATS ASSISTANT . . . . Vicky Ngoma

BIOGRAPHIES OF THE
ORIGINAL STORY TEAM

J.K. ROWLING

is the author of the seven Harry Potter novels, which have sold over 450 million copies and have been translated into 79 languages, and three companion books originally published for charity. She is also the author of *The Casual Vacancy*, a novel for adults published in 2012, and, under the pseudonym of Robert Galbraith, is the author of the Cormoran Strike crime series. J.K. Rowling is making her screen-writing debut and is a producer on the film *Fantastic Beasts and Where to Find Them*, a further extension of the wizarding world, due for release in November 2016.

JOHN TIFFANY

directed the stage adaptation of *Once* for which he was the recipient of multiple awards both in the West End and on Broadway. As Associate Director of the Royal Court, his work includes *The Twits*, *Hope*, and *The Pass*. He was the director of *Let the Right One In* for the National Theatre of Scotland, which transferred to the Royal Court, West End, and St. Ann's Warehouse. His other work for the National Theatre of Scotland includes *Macbeth* (also Broadway), *Enquirer*, *The Missing*, *Peter Pan*, *The House of Bernarda Alba*, *Transform Caithness: Hunter*, *Be Near Me*, *Nobody Will Ever Forgive Us*, *The Bacchae*, *Black Watch*, for which he won the Olivier and Critics Circle Best Director Awards, *Elizabeth Gordon Quinn*, and *Home: Glasgow*. Other recent credits include *The Glass Menagerie* at American Repertory Theatre and on Broadway and *The Ambassador* at the Brooklyn Academy of Music. Tiffany was Associate Director of the National Theatre of Scotland from 2005 to 2012, and was a Radcliffe Fellow at Harvard University in the 2010–2011 academic year.

JACK THORNE

writes for theater, film, television, and radio. His theater credits include *Hope* and *Let the Right One In*, both directed by John Tiffany, *The Solid Life of Sugar Water* for the Graeae Theatre Company and the National Theatre, *Bunny* for the Edinburgh Festival Fringe, *Stacy* for the Trafalgar Studios, and *2nd May 1997* and *When You Cure Me* for the Bush. His adaptations include *The Physicists* for the Donmar Warehouse and *Stuart: A Life Backwards* for HighTide. On film his credits include *War Book*, *A Long Way Down*, and *The Scouting Book for Boys*. For television his credits include *The Last Panthers*, *Don't Take My Baby*, *This Is England*, *The Fades*, *Glue*, *Cast-Offs*, and *National Treasure*. He won 2016 BAFTAs for Best Mini-Series (*This Is England '90*) and Best Single Drama (*Don't Take My Baby*), and in 2012 won Best Drama Series (*The Fades*) and Best Mini-Series (*This Is England '88*).